The Headland

The Headland

Abi Curtis

Goldsmiths
Press

Printed and bound by Short Run Press Limited, UK
Distribution by the MIT Press
Cambridge, Massachusetts, USA and London, England

A CIP record for this book is available from the British Library

ISBN 978-1-915983-12-1 (pbk)
ISBN 978-1-915983-11-4 (ebk)

www.gold.ac.uk/goldsmiths-press

For Gabriel & Dexter

"Full fathom five thy father lies;
Of his bones are coral made;
Those are pearls that were his eyes:
Nothing of him that doth fade,
But doth suffer a sea-change
Into something rich and strange."

William Shakespeare,
The Tempest, 1611

"Love, all alike, no season knows nor clime,
Nor hours, days, months, which are the rags of time."
John Donne, 1633

"It is the stillest words that bring the storm."
Friedrich Nietzsche, 1908

"Earlier on today apparently a woman rang the BBC and
said she had heard that there was a hurricane on the way.
Well, if you are watching, don't worry, there isn't."
Michael Fish, BBC Weather,
15th October 1987

The Headland: 15th October 1987

A storm is coming.

Two men wander along the shingle beach at night, their arms draped over each other's shoulders. They are singing "With or Without You" in high voices. They are brothers. They spent the evening in the Hope and Anchor drinking beer, talking about their childhoods and plotting a Christmas party. Solomon, the elder brother, is a fisherman. The younger, Sebastian, works at the nuclear power station which glows in the distance beyond the cottages on the coast. Each house on the Headland is different: studios converted from old railway carriages, white clapboard, tarred timber. The lighthouse scopes the huge waves, and the wind is strong, getting stronger. They both know the coast of France is out there, not very far and visible quite often, but not tonight. Solomon, who knows the seas and the tides, lifts his head to look at the horizon. Something's up; this is more than just a storm. He's drunk, so not as worried as he should be. Sebastian is looking inland. He's even drunker, stumbling against his brother. They both chuckle.

"Come back to mine, sleep on the sofa," says Solomon. "I don't like the look of that storm."

"Sure, sure, good idea." But Sebastian breaks away from his brother's arm and stalks up the beach towards something that has caught his eye. A dark, irregular shape glows against the shingle. It is quite a way from him, past Solomon's faded white cottage.

"Where are you going?" Solomon shouts above the storm, which is whipping up, howling through the gaps in the dwellings. The waves are thirty feet high, ghosting like walls of water out at sea.

"I can see something, it's bright, maybe…"

"Leave it, Seb," says Solomon, suddenly sobering up, cold spray on his face. A crab net bowls past them on the shingle, propelled by the gale. Sebastian is ahead of him, wind pushing back his anorak and the fabric of his jeans; he's leaning into it in order to walk.

"It's only over there. Bit of driftwood; maybe it's caught fire."

"If it has, it'll soon be out," says Solomon. His voice is snatched away. "Come to the house," he tries to shout, "I don't think it's safe out here. It's really getting up."

The wind screams, the waves roar; Solomon doesn't remember a storm like this. His brother is stubborn and tries to keep walking, reaching his hands towards the object. Then, out of the dark, as if conjured, a metal drum, an empty container from God-knows-where, flies past his ear, just missing his head, crashing onto the shingle with a metallic boom and rolling away. Solomon reaches Sebastian and grabs his arm. He turns and looks back, face pale, eyes wide, stopped dead.

"Alright." He smiles. "Let's get inside before I get brained."

They struggle up to the cottage, wrestling to open the door, then it takes them both to close it behind them. The windowpanes flex and moan as though they might shatter, and the clapboard cracks. Solomon pours two whiskies. Neither brother will sleep tonight. Both will stay downstairs watching TV until the picture pings and turns black. They will listen to the storm rage, wondering how the Headland will be in the morning. Sebastian will spend a while at the window looking at the power station, sipping his whisky, the lines between the pylons singing like the strings of a wayward violin.

THE HEADLAND: THIS SUMMER

A white car weaves along the quiet coastal road from the tiny town of Gold Stone, past converted bungalows and contemporary beach houses with floor-to-ceiling glass, clapboard houses and low-rise flats. The soft, wide sandy beach gives way to flinty shingle. The road bends away from its closeness to the harsh, silver sea, over the tracks of the narrow-gauge railway, past the Hope and Anchor gourmet fish restaurant, and along the Headland's main road, black tarmac edged by shingle, clustered with holiday lets: converted lookouts; a redesigned tannery, and centuries-old fishermen's cottages. The car passes a green and white artist's studio and gallery at the crossroads, a fresh crab van; abandoned and barnacled fishing boats; rusted anchors and plane propellers, and bright yellow JCBs for smoothing the shingle back, chasing the tide which continually moves the stones down the shoreline. The coast of France shimmers across the water like a mirage. The flat land wobbles, the power station hazy in the distance, pylons sketching the landscape beyond it. The narrow-gauge train clatters by, its driver grey with soot, children hanging their heads from the windows. The car stops outside a striking cottage, its timbers stained black, with bright yellow window frames, and a curious overgrown garden of driftwood, herbs and flowers. Seakale is everywhere in the borderless plot, and all over the beach, ripe with the smell of honey, and purple viper's bugloss flowers are scattered over the shingle like something from another planet. That anything grows out of the baking stones in the salty, hot breeze seems a miracle.

The car parks outside the black house, two wheels on the shingle and two on the road, and Morgan Poole climbs out. Morgan is approaching forty, his dark hair is greying around the ears, and when he lets his beard grow (which is not often) it is almost silver. The car is small and low for his rangy frame, and as he stands, he unfolds his long arms and legs and bends back into a stretch. He has always been tall and lanky, floating above everyone else. He doesn't know where his height comes from. The hot breeze hits him after a couple of hours in the air-conditioning, but the briny smell of the sea beats the smell of the car seat and his own sweat. He looks over at his mother's summer house, recalling it from childhood holidays, from weekends, and from a few months ago when she asked him to have lunch with her here instead of in town. This is the landscape of Morgan's childhood: flat, shingled, shimmering in the harsh light. Industrial and decorated with tenacious wildflowers. Beaten to gold by salt and sun.

Morgan is here because his mother has died. He is here to lay claim to the cottage known as Watchbell House, and to attend her funeral. He is also here with a question that he hopes will be answered. He doesn't feel old enough to do this: organise the marking of the end of his mother's life, but there is nobody else. He promised her he would do it. How much is Watchbell worth? Should he sell it, or rent it out? The quirky dwellings that fringe the Headland's coast are always in demand. He finds a bottle of water in the glove compartment and leans against the car, glugging it. He must drive into town to see his mother's solicitor, get the keys to Watchbell, and do what he needs to do. A week or so, he'd told Maggie. He isn't that far if she needs him.

"I'm a bit nervous to be left on my own, to be honest," she said.

"It's a couple of hours away; I can get back easily."

Maggie, ten years younger, working on her PhD in physics. Maggie with her beautiful body and glossy brown bob, who was just meant to be a few months of fun. He likes her, sure he does, the girl from the Science Department coming to history lectures just for interest, whip-smart, funny, doing something brilliant with quantum stuff he doesn't pretend to understand, sexy as hell. He thinks of her: soft and gorgeous, lying in bed on Sunday mornings with the curtains open, dust motes playing in the early light, the sound of city traffic in the street below. Morgan was drawn to Maggie when he first met her. They'd eat lunch in the university canteen and between mouthfuls of ramen she'd tell him about her research. Most of it was too complex to understand. She was fascinated by quantum time, how time couldn't be linear, how it was just a slice of it that people perceived. She bought him a donut and sliced into it to illustrate the point. The jam oozed out and she dipped a finger in. "Not the jam though; that doesn't represent anything." He'd laughed and licked it off her finger in a gesture obscenely intimate for his workplace. He'd tried to resist her, but was always drawn back. His skin hummed when she was close to him, as though she had a field around her. Gradually, they spent more and more time together.

But now he is in trouble. Maggie is pregnant. A human being made of his and her DNA would ground Morgan in the world. He is trapped. Maggie is no longer his physical comfort; she is a responsibility. He sees his own childhood as he gazes out at the Headland's shoreline, his small form walking on the sunlit beach. His fatherless self.

It just isn't what he had planned for; he isn't ready for it. Children have never been in his vision of the future. She isn't ready either, but she is full of practical bravado, trying to take it in her stride.

"I can take some maternity leave; the funders will let me extend the project. If we rent somewhere a bit bigger together, get out of our own flats, then…There's a nursery attached to the uni, so…"

But as the birth gets closer, he sees her panicking, staying at work late to immerse herself in the research. She won't join any antenatal classes, and he certainly isn't going to any. "Bunch of hippy mums…just give me all the drugs, I say, or a C-section, better still," she laughs. But he's caught her looking at soft little baby-grows in shop windows, or eyeing prams being pushed along the high street. And Morgan, he is not a parent. No. He surely cannot be. He sees himself, for a moment, through his mother's eyes from her bed in palliative care, gently closing the door. Why create someone else he will have to say goodbye to? Maggie and the child will do better without him. He must find a way to make Maggie understand this.

This trip is a break for Morgan, time to think about his dead mother and being her son. He'd never told her about the baby, as if by not mentioning it, it may not come to pass. She'd never met Maggie, though Maggie had asked many times.

"She's not really fit for visitors – she's really gone downhill health-wise now. I don't want to excite her."

"But won't she be pleased, to know you are having a child?"

"I think it will just make her sad, you know, thinking she'll just miss being a grandparent…"

Maggie didn't push the point.

Morgan sighs and gets back in the car, and weaves his way along the coast towards town, passing the power station as he goes. A small group of protestors gather at the gates. *Stop the closure of nuclear power,* begs one of the placards. Hardly a catchy slogan, but Morgan has read the story: the station is due to close next year despite protests that nuclear energy is carbon neutral and one of the only clean options left. He's not sure they'll get very far – others are still afraid of the consequences of an accident, and of the waste buried in the sea. He still has a few hours until the sun goes down. Hopefully, he'll have the keys by then and can sit in the porch of Watchbell House with a cold beer and start to wrap things up.

The entrance to the solicitor's office on the high street is squeezed between a jewellery shop and a bakery whose window is piled with garish cupcakes. It's cool and dark in the building's medieval staircase and it smells of wood polish. The receptionist directs him with a wave of her hand, and Morgan ducks under an exposed beam, into a short corridor, and to the solicitor's door. A brass plaque declares "Germain Jones: Solicitor" as if anyone else might be there. For a moment, Jones doesn't look up from the file in front of him. His office is modern inside, with a clean metal desk, grey carpet, and bright white walls, at odds with the low ceilings, nooks and sloping floors of the building. Jones has dull ginger hair, curly but cut very short, freckled skin, and a long nose. There is something feline about his face. He looks up and gestures for Morgan to sit opposite him. He has a cardboard shoebox, tied with a frayed purple ribbon, sitting incongruously on the elegant desk. His handshake is firm, and his voice so very deep that Morgan looks quickly around the room as if someone else has spoken. Morgan returns the grip, feeling sweaty and dull from the day's journey.

"I'm sorry for your loss, Mr Poole."

"Thank you; I appreciate that."

"Did the receptionist offer you tea, coffee?"

"No, but it's okay."

Jones rolls his eyes. "She never does. I only ask because one day life might surprise me." He leans back in his Eames chair, gazing at the cloudless sky out of the window. A seagull lands on the sill and starts to peck and worry at the paint-work. Jones raises an eyebrow but turns back to Morgan.

"There's a bit of paperwork to do, but everything is left to you in the will, as you might imagine. Then a few things your mother wanted you to have. The funeral is arranged, as you know. One of her friends –" he flips over a notepad – "Randy Peterson, she's taking care of the finer details."

"At Café Ferdinand?"

"Yes. She owns the place, but she doesn't run it anymore. Your mother, Dolores, felt it would be good to have a local do the catering and co-ordinate things."

Morgan remembers Randy's café from summers spent at the Headland, running in barefoot for strawberry ice cream, toes sandy from the cluster of dunes above the sharp shingle beach, the bell clanging.

"So, property-wise," Jones brings out a thick document, "the flat on Second Avenue has sold…"

"It's sold? I didn't realise it was on the market."

"Dolores didn't want you to worry about it. And she wanted the bills for her care covered. It was snapped up – on the market for a day, literally. Once it's all gone through, the remaining proceeds are yours of course. I'll arrange the transfer. There's always a small fee, but…"

Second Avenue. The flat where he'd been brought up before he left for university, where they'd crammed into the bath together when he was little, watered window boxes of tomato plants, burnt the toast and watched Saturday night TV and Sunday morning music videos. Morgan takes a breath. Jones pushes a set of keys across the table.

"She was keen for you to have Watchbell House – the Headland house. That's the property that meant something to her." Morgan feels the cool metal of the keys and runs their sharpness over his hot fingertips.

"Can I sell it?"

Jones's eyes flicker across the document, "She didn't stipulate anywhere here that you couldn't. It's yours to do with what you choose. And here," Jones pushes the cardboard shoebox, on its side the word *Clarks* almost completely faded, across the desk. "She wanted you to have the documents in this box; they were important to her. And a letter that explains."

"Have you read this?" asks Morgan. The letter is in a thin, white envelope, clean and new in contrast to the tatty old box.

"No, of course not." Jones offers him a smile. "It's addressed to you. Have you any questions, Mr Poole?"

"Actually, I…" Morgan leans back in his chair and for a moment they both observe the seagull, still peeling the paintwork off the windowsill and flaking it into the street below. Jones's expression is neutral; he doesn't seem bothered by the slow demolition of his window. Perhaps he once did but it happens every day, and there is no solution and he has accepted it as a fact of life. Morgan leans in.

"Did she leave anything, or say anything, about my father?"

"Your father?" Jones turns away from the seagull and leans his elbows on the desk, flicking through the paperwork again. "She was married at one stage. Otherwise, there's nothing here. Perhaps the documents in your box there… They aren't legal documents, but she said they were personal. Or perhaps the letter…" His face remains impassive, as if the seagull shows his agitation for him.

Morgan is desperate now to open the box with the old ribbon, and the letter growing sweaty in his hands. He has asked a few times about his father over the years. As a child, his mother would say, "We get on fine, just the two of us, don't we? I love you enough for ten people." After a nasty argument in his teens, where he screamed at her that she didn't know who his father was, she looked at him sadly and said, "A mother always knows where her child comes from. But it was always just you and me. It wasn't possible for there to be anyone else. I had friends to help me. Sometimes life isn't quite what you imagine it is going to be, but that doesn't make it bad." After a while, he realised that perhaps his mother didn't know his father well, or that he had not been a good man, and he stopped asking. But now that he is supposed to be a father himself...

"Mr Poole, let's get you that coffee, shall we? Then we can sign off this paperwork. I'm sure you're keen to get on."

2nd May

Dearest Morgan,

*It seems odd to be writing this letter, from beyond the grave
as it were. Not everyone has the chance to know when they
are going to die, and even though I don't know the exact
date, I know it's going to be soon. And I know you and I
have talked, but there are some other things I wanted to say.
No doubt you've seen Germain Jones. Curious fellow, my
solicitor, but very good. He'll sort everything. I don't want
you to worry about money, or the nurses' bills or anything
at all. Randy and I have planned me a nice send-off and I
know Randy will be so pleased to see you again all grown up.*

*So, you've got an old shoe box. Quite the legacy! But inside
you are going to find a journal that I kept over just one year,
a strange year in my life. I found the box sorting through
my stuff, getting ready to say goodbye to it all. I had almost
forgotten about that year – the details of it anyway. As time
goes on, the memories crop up less and less often. But they
are always with me. I suppose you just get on with things,
and they fade into the background. But I found it and read
it through, and I wanted to share with you something I have
never talked about, my only real secret. So that is in the
pages of the journal.*

*Your birth was shortly after and swept everything away. I
didn't think I could love anyone so much, my beautiful boy.
When I first saw your face, it was as if I had known you all
my life. Of course; it's you! And we got along just fine, you*

and I in the little flat on Second Avenue, and on the beach in the summers. Until you got older, and I don't think it was cool anymore – the city was more exciting. And so it should be. I'm so proud of you, Morgan. You had a sorrowful, serious little face as a baby, and I think you're serious now. But that's okay; just don't forget to have a chuckle from time to time.

So, the journal you'll find here – I'm not sure how you'll take it but remember it's from a time before you came along and made the world make sense. I'm sorry I had to die sooner than I would have chosen, and that I have had to miss a chunk of your life. It's my only regret. Death isn't so bad for me because I won't be here, but how I would miss you if I were aware in any way.

How I would look across time as if it were a tunnel with you at the other end, that I could never pass through to hold you again. I hope this journal works as a parting gift to you, I hope its story gives you something. In a strange way, and although I did not know it at the time, it is your story.

All my love, my sweet boy,

Mum x

There are hot, painful tears in Morgan's throat. He's on the porch of Watchbell House with a beer as the blazing sun goes down. Inside the box is a pale red exercise book, the kind he used to have at school. It is dog-eared and its pages are filled with his mother's neat handwriting in blue biro. Under that are clippings from newspapers and magazines, so delicate and thin it seems they could crumble in his hands. Surely, inside the journal, he'll discover who his father is. To know that might help him to be a father himself, if be one he must. Watchbell is cool inside, and once the light has gone, he'll go back in and read the journal in the living room, but for now he stays in the porch, opens the journal gently to the first page, and begins.

<u>Friday 16th October 1987.</u>

I am taking to writing in order to explain, in order to try to make sense. Since Adrian isn't here with me anymore, I cannot tell him about the past night and day. I'm not sure he would understand anyway. I'm not sure I understand. And something in me says I should not tell anyone else; not at the moment. Not before I have got my head around it. But to keep a record – to write it down. That seems like the thing to do. And I can tell you; though you are not here with me, somehow, I think that you would have understood. I suppose because your heart and mine are one and the same. So, I address this to you, imagining you might be interested, knowing that you would also have loved this place where I live.

The last twenty-four hours have been extraordinary to say the least. The storm tore around Watchbell House all night. I don't remember a storm like it in my lifetime. I thought the dark wooden planks would simply lift off, off and away out to sea, leaving me exposed in a skinless, skeleton house. The walls rattled and creaked. I thought the wind might come in and pull the pots and pans clean out of the cupboards and scatter them across the beach. Tear up the rug and spin my paints and paintbrushes high into the whipping sky. Then me. Then me, pulled up by the arms like a child. A dream of Oz. I lay all night on the sofa, my bed empty upstairs, the fire continually going out, listening, listening to the screams of the wind, the roar of the waves. How it pulled and prised at the things outside. It seemed to hate something or want something gone.

A great rending. I looked out into the dark, through the rain-lashed window, to my beach garden, to see what might hold on. Plants being dragged out at the root. My carefully placed driftwood, my shells and snatches of flint all battered away. And the roaring of it. The great white smashing of the sea in the darkness. The moon quivered.

I wasn't afraid. I didn't imagine I could ever be afraid again. Not since you. Not on this anniversary. I thought, *Come on; is that all you've got? Show me what you're made of.* I am made of ash and water. Of drifting shingle and snatches of cloud. I am made of the seagull song, sharp and insistent and sad. *Come on; rip the roof off as you might lift off my skull. Show me your mutable, massive face.* I want to make a storm, find a storm inside me. If only. If anything, I wanted more noise, more destruction. So I thought in the dead of night. These were strange thoughts, as if the storm itself drew them out of me.

In the morning, I didn't feel that way. I put the telephone to my ear. Nothing. I peered out of the window. Wotsit, my huge orange cat, was still under the sofa, but a tin of tuna coaxed him out. The wind had calmed to a breeze and the sea, though high and tussling, was almost normal again. I saw pieces of houses strewn about. Papers and plastic bags on the normally clean stone beach. The coastline was grubby with flotsam that the sea had given back. The wrecks of old boats, so picturesque against the skyline, were more wrecked, listing on the shingle and stripped of wood. Figures were emerging, picking their way about, collecting things flown from their unbounded gardens. The TV was dead. I couldn't contact the school, but I knew it would be closed today – my students thrilled and terrified at home. I opened the door and saw the partial destruction of the garden that I had been working on since spring. Purple Michaelmas daisies, still standing but splayed with their petals plucked away, hydrangeas blushed and sun-scorched. The lavender remained but smelled strong, as though in protest. I noticed a green moth fluttering there, its proboscis coiling out, its eyes furred, and its wings ragged. There was still a mist over the sea, and I could not make out the suggestion of France, as I might on a clear day, across the channel. I turned to make a survey of the house itself, to check its tar-coated, black timber cladding. Once a fisherman's cottage, it is tough as old boots against the elements, and it is intact apart from a hairline crack tracing its way down one windowpane like a spider's web. I will have to get this replaced. Gulls lifted and wheeled about in the spent currents of the wind. There was a spit of rain and a feeling of remorse in the fresh, pale grey scraps of cloud.

My plan was to go to Café Ferdinand, out on the edge of the beach near the old lighthouse and the entrance to the narrow-gauge railway line. I wondered about damage to these. I wondered if people might congregate there and discuss what needed to be put right and repaired. Perhaps Randy would have a working TV or phone. I saw the phone lines, criss-crossing the artists' studios, coastguard cottages and converted railway carriages, the mixture of hangouts, residences and holiday cottages. Some of the lines dangled, loosely, like the broken strings of instruments played too hard. There were two figures in the distance walking down the beach, but I walked away from them. I didn't want to talk yet. I was still held in the breath of the storm. My voice felt silenced in the landscape. I wasn't disturbed then by the thought of the destruction. I saw, as I walked and listened to the sea's drag, that large, oblong flints had been uncovered by the storm. I thought, I suppose inappropriately, I would collect these later for the garden and stick them up like teeth amongst the elder bushes. There are no walls or fences around my garden, only the bounds of the horizon. I looked back at my little cottage, black, mostly intact, its two windows and front door painted primrose-yellow, its chimney sticking straight up. A child's painting of a house.

I took off down the beach, flint crunching, the power station emerging from the mist ahead of me. It looms strangely in this sun-blasted shingle desert. A blue light was flashing nearby, and for a moment I wondered if the storm had threatened the reactor. What a prospect. People are still terrified after Chernobyl blew last year. Worries about cancer and their babies being born deformed. If anything ever happened, this whole region and most of the city would be uninhabitable for decades. You can't think too much about it. If something was wrong with the reactor, there would already have been evacuations, a siren crying for us to leave. But I imagine in the howling night how those in charge must have felt. So, there I was. Walking on this weird morning after a great storm we were told by the weatherman would not occur. My home was safe, the sea had calmed, the mist was burning away, and I was headed to Café Ferdinand along the Headland to see if Randy had a working phone, a TV signal. Pieces of litter and wood strewn about. Damage assessments taking place.

Then I see and am drawn to a large piece of driftwood. It is deeply grained, smoothed over by countless years at sea. If I didn't know better, I'd say it was a pine, but such wood is too soft to survive. It was oak, I'm sure, but morphed by the sea's caress; greenish, smelling of brine, thoroughly coated in barnacles along one edge, like hundreds of tiny eyes. It was as long as my leg and as thick, tapered at one end. There were many twisted sections like muscle fibres. In the middle: a layered, mouth-shaped hole. Why, I don't know, but I stopped there. I thought the driftwood particularly beautiful. It had a calm, sculptural elegance about it in the aftermath of the storm. However, the storm must have brought it here – I have never seen it before and I have often collected driftwood. But I also had a weird feeling it had been there, embedded in the shingle, for all time, and that I had just never noticed, that the storm had made me see it. I knew I wanted it for the garden, to lay it out amongst the tenacious borage, that it would make a striking feature. I also knew I would have to come back after my visit to Café Ferdinand to get it. I couldn't drag it around. I peered into the hole. The smell that came back was fishy, like the slick scent of an oyster, but had a trace of lemons and smoke about it too. I felt disgust, as I never normally do with fish: a nausea that made me draw away. At the same time, I wanted to smell it again, to keep smelling it.

I heard a sound, "Click, click," like someone tutting or encouraging a horse. I placed my hand on the wood, and it was warm to the touch. Warm as toast. And it vibrated. But I could see nothing inside. The edges of the woody hole were clear, and I saw into the textured back of the log, pale and striped with its previous growth. I stood back a moment, wondering about my state of mind. I had not eaten breakfast, which accounted for the nausea and lightness in my head, the vibrations. The wood was gorgeous as a rediscovered wreck, smooth as a limb. I wanted it for my garden. It must have caught the warmth of the sun and felt hot against the cold skin of my hands. That was all. It vibrated in the breeze, still jittery from the storm. I put my hand inside the hole, to get a grip and feel its heft for later on when I would take it home. I put a hand inside, and everything changed.

This is not what Morgan is expecting. There is the odd sense of an addressee – it can't be him as the journal is dated before his existence, and yet at moments it feels as though he is being told directly, as if time had collapsed. There is the mention of someone called Adrian, but his mother doesn't say who he is and why he isn't there. All her focus seems to be on the beach, the storm, the discovery of a piece of wood. She doesn't talk about his father, or any other hint of a secret. Morgan is being impatient; there are months of the diary to go. He teaches history; he ought to be used to trawling through first-hand documents, reading hundreds of pages looking for one piece of evidence. His eyes are straining in the dark, so he goes inside and sets up the coffee pot on the old stove. There are a few things in the cupboard, sugar, teabags, tinned food and spices, a gummed-up bottle of malt vinegar. His phone is flashing on the counter, but he doesn't touch it. He turns on the lamp next to the sofa and drinks his coffee black with three sugars and a stale custard cream. Above the fireplace hangs one of his mother's huge canvases, perhaps one of the biggest she ever painted, a black abstract shape catching the light like velvet or tar, resting on the oak table with the window frame in the background. No view is painted in the window. When he looks at the painting, his head feels light. The real table is still here, under the window, beyond it a view of the power station and the deepening night sky. His mother rarely painted still lives, and when she did, they were in oils rather than her usual watercolours. He loved it, as a child, when the oil paints came out of their folding box, smelling of potatoes, greasy and messy, half-squeezed

tubes of reds and greens, muddy browns and burning yellows. He'll keep this painting; it will look good in his flat.
The flat Maggie thinks they should sell. He sits on the sofa
and continues to read.

I thought at first that my hand had touched nothing, just the salty damp of the inside of the driftwood, but then I felt a vibration against my skin, the tiny hairs at the back of my hand rising up; something warm on me; my pores registering. For a moment I felt warm skin, creamy, slick as a seal. Something touched me and I touched it back, but then it was also gone, not-there. I cannot explain it any other way than this: there was something alive inside that hollowed driftwood and it had touched me for a moment, and then it phased away and was no longer there. I have tried to explain it to myself all day. I thought perhaps if I wrote it down this evening, I might be able to…But no words quite fit. I felt a kind of terror, thinking for a moment that my hand had been painlessly severed. I drew it out and stumbled back. I moved my fingers, now cooling, around. I was unharmed. Intact. I looked inside the darkness of the log, rolling it back so the light would catch it. I could see nothing inside. So I left it there. It had unsettled me. I decided against taking it back for the garden. But as I walked on, I could not stop thinking about it. I headed along the beach, roughly following the tracks of the narrow-gauge railway, on my way to Café Ferdinand, which sat sheltered behind a tufted dune. As I did, I saw a beach house with its side ripped away by the storm, just as if some huge creature had taken a bite. Plaster and the frayed edges of wallpaper hung from the edges. The wallpaper had a pattern of hot air balloons. I saw the layers of the floors, broken pipes still gushing water. This was the most serious damage I'd seen, and it jolted me out of what had seemed like a dream muffled by the wind. I realised the destruction I had escaped and thanked Watchbell House, my ancient fisherman's cottage, for its squat strength. I also knew, and thought darkly, of the woman who lived in the damaged house: Irene, Seb and Solomon's grandmother. I hoped with all my heart that she was okay and had not been in that room that no longer was.

Café Ferdinand is pale blue and cream clapboard with a hand-painted sign above the door. Randy, its owner, does a fabulous trade in the summer, especially the gelato in its pastel-coloured tubs (you would have loved that, I know). But even in the off-season the locals come for bacon butties, dark and steaming tea, and toasted teacakes, blackened at the edges and loaded with jam. Randy had another life before she came to the Headland. She was a country singer, but the people back in Lubbock, Texas, didn't take to the fact that she hasn't always been a woman, and when they discovered it, they made life difficult. She ended up here amongst the artists' studios and the tourists on the beach and realised they needed a café. She is so well loved by the community here that nobody dares to say a word against her. I went into the café, hoping for a working radio, or news from the television above the counter. The café was empty but for Seb and Solomon, sitting across from one another at a wooden table. Solomon was facing me, his black hair with its wild curls dipping over one eye, a steaming mug beside him. He was lifting a bacon butty up to his mouth but lowered it back to the plate when he saw me. His brother, Seb, whose back was to me, swivelled his head. Both brothers have eyes the colour of flint and hair as black a guillemots, but where Solomon has a mop of curls, Seb's hair is grass-straight and he keeps it short and gelled. Solomon was in his fisherman's overalls and I noticed his eyes were bloodshot. The café was silent. Seb nodded and turned back around.

"You want a cuppa, Dolly?" Randy stood up from where she'd been hidden, bent under the counter, trying to fix the radio. I nodded, unwrapping my scarf. The TV was dark, the radio silent. "Are you alright? The cottage okay?" Randy's Texan accent has softened over the years and is edged with a south-coast laziness. I went over and stood close as Randy handed over my tea. The enamel cup was hot to the touch; I recalled the strange warmth inside the driftwood and had that urge to go back.

"It's fine," I told her. "Nothing really damaged. I'm lucky."

"Want something to eat? Bacon butty? Scrambled egg? Thank goodness for the gas stove."

I was hungry but I shook my head. It's hard to eat these days. Everything sticks in my throat. As if there are words in there that I haven't yet said, blocking the way. Randy is tall and sturdy, I think at least six feet, with beautiful cheekbones and her copper hair piled high. I have never seen her without plum-coloured lips and three coats of mascara. She leaned over the counter and whispered to me,

"Irene died in the night, in the storm. They've just come from the hospital."

The news I had dreaded when I saw the side of her little house blown clean away. The storm had not simply passed over. It had taken things, and people, as it went. I looked down at the knots on the wooden counter – reclaimed like the tables and chairs. Wood from wrecked boats and uprooted oaks. I tried to see a pattern in the dark whorls, but there was none. I didn't know what to say to Seb or Solomon, who sat silently over their breakfasts. Irene had been in her nineties. I often saw her tending her beach garden. She once gave me some cuttings for my own. I don't have a grandmother anymore, but if I did, she would be precious.

"Gentlemen, would you like more tea?" said Randy then, which was at least something.

Solomon is the older brother – a fisherman – he had on his overalls but peeled half-down so they just looked like trousers, a thick grey jumper over his torso, and a stone with a natural hole in the centre suspended from a gold chain around his neck. He got up and came to the counter, stood at my side and nodded. I told him I was sorry. So sorry, I think I said, and I saw him swallow.

"They don't think she knew much. She would have just fallen, from the bedroom, and then there was lots of debris. It would be like being caught in a demolition, I suppose. We've been up all night, just, just because…"

I saw then that he was pale, despite his sun-blushed skin, with a shadow of stubble across his chin. He's a little older than me, maybe nearer forty, and we don't talk much, but I've always liked the careful way he speaks. I like to watch him go out silently on his boat and come back in. His daughter, Claire, is in my class, and she's good at collage and drawing. I love teaching her; she is always willing to experiment. I know he doesn't see her as much as he'd like to. He bought one of my paintings once; I had no idea he even liked my work, but it may have been because his fishing boat was in the background. It's a painting of the shingle beach, my attempt to capture the deep purple of the sunset, the ochre and grey of a storm on its way, the creamy waves blasting against the shore.

"Make it a strong tea, Randy," he said. I went to touch his arm, where he leant on the counter at my side, but thought better of it. He said Irene's funeral would be next week.

Seb was not usually as quiet as Solomon but today he said little, staring at the scrubby grass that grows on the dunes and was still blustering in what was left of the wind. Solomon handed him another tea and he pushed his empty cup away.

"I'll have to go to work soon," he said. He works at the power station. I wondered if he ought to have been there earlier, but I suppose they let him come late, given the night they had spent. The mechanisms tick on, no matter what happens. Randy told us she still couldn't get a radio signal, twizzling through the buzz of static. She said to try the Community Centre perhaps. I guessed that as the morning wore on, people would congregate here at the café for

Randy's warmth and good food. I didn't want to stay for them, so I told Seb and Solomon to come to the cottage if they needed me to help with anything. I was thinking all the time of the driftwood, and how, after all, I would go back and take it home. I didn't even know why, but leaving it there seemed irresponsible, careless as the storm itself.

Friday 16th October 1987, 2 a.m.

I'm on the sofa writing this, Wotsit draped over my feet. I don't want to go up to my bed; the events of the day have unsettled me so much. Wotsit's eyes are shut like two stitches in his sweet face, his whiskers fine viola strings. There is still a wind flustering at the window, but the storm is over. After I visited Café Ferdinand, I went to the Community Centre. Across the street a tree had fallen onto a car, shattering its windscreen in a crush of white glass. The Centre is a temporary building put up in the sixties, still solid now with a low roof and corrugated walls. They gave me candles and matches and canned food for the stove, which I stashed in the deep pockets of my tin cloth coat. They said the electricity might be out for a week. The place was being run by two women from the post office and Tony, the vicar. He smiled at me, but always finds it hard making eye contact. I am too much for some people it seems, even those that are supposed to hear God. And God has always struck me as quite challenging. I, for one, would not like to be on his direct line. But it is what they see in me, I think, that some find it hard to face. Tony told

me the electricity might be out for a week, and I have still
not seen the TV or heard the radio.

I made my way back along the beach, the power station
at my back. That was the thing everyone wanted to talk
about. They feared a meltdown. I'm not sure what one
would look like. I picture the reactor burning white and
blue and everything melting like wax. People's skin falling
off in sheets. But that may just be my morbid imagination.
The station's lights were on, its workers no doubt caring
for it into the evening, and I expect through the night. As
I walked along the shingle, I saw Irene's partial house, a
van parked outside with a stranger loading rubble into the
back, the shadow of Solomon talking to him. He did not
see me. I understand this: you have to keep tidying up,
even when someone is lost, gone forever. You have to keep
what is left neat.

I tracked back along the shingle to Watchbell House. At
first, I could not see the driftwood and thought it was gone,
moved or taken by someone. I was surprised by the stab of
panic I felt in my chest, as though I had failed to protect it.
Then I saw its grey shape, like a risen shadow, still in the
distance on the shingle where I had left it; it was just further
away than I remembered. As it came into view, it looked
slightly different to the image I had kept all morning in my
mind, more ordinary and inert. It was cold to the touch,
still beautifully knotted and skin-smooth, still hollowed
out. I lifted it. It was dense and heavy as a sack of flour or a
terracotta pot. I tilted it to look into the hole and saw nothing; it only caught the pale glow of the sun for a moment. I

did not put my hand inside this time. It was heavy enough that I had to carry it across both arms, stopping to adjust it and rest often on my short walk back. Dragging it would have been best, but I did not want to damage it, tough as it felt, and even though it had spent so long at sea. I wanted to be gentle. Sweat prickled across my arms and chest. I felt stupid – though the beach was empty – in the way I felt stupid when I returned from the supermarket with more bags than I could carry, having stubbornly avoided the bus fare. I made it to my unfenced garden and carried it up to the front door, the door I painted "Permanent Yellow no. 664" because I liked the name of the colour so much. Permanent, always, never-changing yellow. Wotsit was curled over a stone I sometimes use to prop open the door in summer, drawn to its warmth. His back arched at the sight of the driftwood. I thought for a moment that he was spooked; I'd never seen him do this. But he sauntered over to where it rested on the step and purred, rubbing his flanks against it as he often does with my legs.

"Silly puss," I said, fumbling with keys and letting us in.

I emptied my pockets of candles and matches and tinned spaghetti hoops. I clattered those onto the table and lugged the driftwood in and lifted that too onto the table. Its wood was pale and silvery compared to the knotted oak beneath it. Wotsit jumped onto the sofa back, kneaded its fabric with his paws, and was watchful after that.

I suppose I didn't know what to do. It looked just like a piece of driftwood that would make a pretty sculpture for Watchbell's garden. It was inert: a dead tree. Had I imagined everything this morning? My thoughts are not what they once were. They are haphazard, unclear and not to be trusted. Painters need an imagination, don't they? Whilst I paint real scenes, the beach, the changing light of the sky, even the suggestion of France on the clearest day, I also must use my imagination whilst I do it. I think of how someone in France might be looking back towards my coast and seeing different shades. Cobalt Green, Bismuth Yellow, Titanium White. I try to stroke the brushes over the damp paper in a way that is mindful of the temperature of the breeze on my skin, the honey scent of the sea-kale and its colour somewhere between Permanent Mauve and Mars Violet. I want to create textures and hues that the viewer might almost feel...

But my latest painting is half-finished and has been on its easel in the upstairs room for just over a year. I feel guilty often, in front of my pupils, encouraging them to paint whilst knowing I don't anymore myself. A terrible fraud. I wonder if my imagination is just buzzing, pent-up and directing itself wherever it can. If this is the start of it: a kind of madness, the first example of which is driftwood come to life.

I set up the blue kettle on the stove and waited for its plaintive whistle. I made a strong, sweet tea and I sat with the wood and thought of sketching its shape with a pale wash of Raw Sienna. I saw the brush repeating its curves, its sinews, of shading its central, whorled hole. But I did not do it. I did not touch a brush. I fed Wotsit instead. The sun started to go down and I placed a hand on the wood. My hand was warm from the mug I held, but the wood seemed to take the warmth from my skin, leaving it chilled. I traced my hand over the wood's smooth surface and the warmth spread. Wotsit darted suddenly under the sofa. I felt vibrations again, now all over the surface of the wood. They began as a kind of itching, like a swarm of insects too small to see, crawling quickly over, then the movement settled into a low, charged quiver. I moved back, tempted again to put my hand inside, but so afraid I half rose from my chair. For a second, from the corner of my eye as I turned to seek out Wotsit's shadow from under the sofa, I saw a brief, iridescent flash from the hole, as if a light were being shone into it. But I had not lit the candles and was sitting in the dark blue dusk as it deepened. I looked directly and again it was there. I have never been a brave person, even when forced, but I moved close, sat back down, and brought my eye to look directly into the hole as if staring into a diorama, closing my other eye. I caught its scent, briny, smoky, with hint of lemon and something richer like chocolate. I looked deep inside at the rings of the tree's previous life, and this time I saw something. A picture resolving.

Adrian once brought home an autostereogram, a geometric picture of dots and lines. It was a clever optical illusion, a parlour trick. I had to look at it in a certain way, he said, and the two-dimensional picture would reveal a three-dimensional image. I couldn't see this hidden picture, and he was so pleased with himself that he could, and I could not.

"Look *through* the image, that's the trick. It's about getting the eyes to focus differently."

All afternoon I was frustrated looking at this thing. Trying to see. Then I put it up to my nose so that I could barely see it at all and moved it slowly away. It resolved suddenly into an image of a butterfly which rose from the paper and seemed to move. It was so strangely always there, and my eyes were so out of focus that I could see nothing at all in my own world. I whooped in delight at my new seeing, and Adrian, in the other room, laughed out loud. I can only describe looking into the driftwood as the same: now that my eye was close, I could see something. I almost *felt* it with my eye. I wondered if, unlike the autostereogram, which depends on depth-perception, two eyes converging, this might depend on closing one eye and could only be seen in two dimensions. Had I accidentally realised the trick?

What I saw was heart-shaped, with myriad legs or tendrils emanating from it. These were coiling and uncoiling so rapidly and so dynamically connected to the heart shape that I could not see how many there were. Perhaps twenty, perhaps a hundred. They were both insect-like and plant-like, shiny and phasing through the full colour spectrum, then disappearing altogether, perhaps as my eye lost its skill, though it seemed to me they somehow existed both here and elsewhere at the same time. The heart shape also shone, as if made of glass, and at its centre was a kind of shifting "stain" that looked the same colour as the wood, brown-grey like sepia, but then changed suddenly from a random blob to a golden-green perfect circle as I stared at it. There was a soft, shushing sound coming from the heart shape, like the breathing of someone peacefully asleep. I knew at that moment that it was a living thing. I understood this from what I saw, what I smelt and heard, but also with a clear and definite thought that came into my head. It was my own thought, but unusually sure. (I have had few trustworthy thoughts for a while.) It was a trust that this weird thing hidden in the deadest of wood was living.

Once I had seen it, it seemed in some way to see me. It drew closer to my eye. I felt repulsed by the intimacy of our meeting, but I kept staring at the perfect green-gold circle on what I will call its "face", how the edges of this shape shimmered and then settled. The shape was familiar to me, and I suddenly realised it was my own eye, the exact shade (my mother and I are the only green-eyed people in the family), and the stain on the creature's surface had altered its shape once it had encountered my eye. I wanted it to watch me, but I was also so afraid to move my heart pulsed.

I drew back and returned to my familiar world, this little dark cottage with its square room and kitchenette, the battered blue kettle and Wotsit hiding under the sofa, the old oat tins on the windowsill holding dry paintbrushes and Michaelmas daisies, and my scrubbed oak table with the driftwood resting there like the subject of a still life.

Funny the moments in your life that you won't realise are turning points until later, that will come back to you over and over. How you'll try to visualise the exact colours; recall what you saw, felt or heard. With these moments you'll always be convinced you have a perfect memory; they are so important, how could you not? So clear as they replay that you may as well be experiencing them for the first time right now. But ask someone else who happened to be there too, and there will be discrepancies: *but he didn't say that, he said...or it wasn't raining, just cloudy, it was a VW, not a Mini-Cooper, a doctor, not a nurse, Friday and not Wednesday...*And so the fierceness of your memory must soften or replay differently. As you tell it to others, you begin to doubt yourself.

But nobody was here tonight but me and a big orange cat who slunk out from under the sofa and climbed up onto the table and sniffed the driftwood. And whatever it was in there came out, slid out...no, somehow oozed out, was iridescent and transparent at the same time, like the skin of a soap bubble. I could only see it slant-wise, closing one eye, concentrating hard on seeing differently in order to perceive it at all. I think Wotsit may be able to see it, or he senses it in other ways, because as it moved, his gaze followed it and he sniffed at the air around it. Its creeping legs shimmered in and out of my vision and the circle that had mimicked my eye disappeared. Now it was a kind of stain again but shifting and morphing into different forms. This stain is the only part of this being that has colour, the only thing my vision can latch on to; when its legs move, they flash colour, but it doesn't stay for more than a second. The stain shifted like iron filings to form two orange triangles that I quickly realised were images of Wotsit's ears. So this is, I think, a kind of mirror, or a mimicking back to those it encounters, though I haven't figured out the purpose. I stood there holding my breath. Because the legs coiled and recoiled so quickly, I had the sense it could viciously strike at any moment at me or Wotsit and perhaps sting us. I found myself holding out my palms and saying, "Shhh…"

One of its limbs uncoiled like the proboscis of an insect, felt towards my arm and rested there. Its touch was light and moist like the catch of a cobweb. It dabbed only my skin, and the stain on its face moved and shifted as its limb felt mine. Again, that creamy coating on its surface. I thought it must be a sea creature, an unusual squid or eel capable of changing shape, but able to exist outside of the water, like a seal. It doesn't make sense. And then I thought about the power station. I do not know what radioactivity does. There are protestors there sometimes, invoking Chernobyl and the mutations it has caused. I know the power is made by splitting the tiniest version of the universe, harnessing the very spin and whirl of time and space. I don't know what it might do to a creature from the Headland's dark seas if it were to be contaminated, if something leaked, if…

My skin prickled. But it did not hurt me. All the time it was on the table, reaching towards us, but I could not say if it needed the table to "stand" on or if it was floating just above it. It went to touch Wotsit next. Before I could think, as one of its limbs touched Wotsit's delicate whiskers, all his fur stood up and he arched his back into a horseshoe and hissed, his tail quivering.

"No, no," I said, and the creature was no longer there. Gone. I squinted. I closed each eye in turn. I saw no weird iridescence or transparent skin, no moving stain, no arms or tentacles or whatever they were. I wondered if Wotsit could have eaten it or shredded it so quickly I didn't see; I have no idea how delicate it is. I peered back inside the driftwood and saw nothing but the knotted lines of the tree.

And here I am now, on the sofa. I got out the old encyclopaedia – thinking perhaps this was indeed a sea creature and it had suddenly dried up and disappeared, a death appropriate to its delicate there-ness. I felt I had failed it. I should have put it in the sink and covered it in cool water. I saw in the encyclopaedia that it shared some characteristics with the mimic octopus: colour changing, probing tentacles that have independent senses. But its legs are many more than eight and they are insect-like somehow, as is the feeling of friability it gave me. And the legs seemed almost to have their own consciousness, never mind their own senses. Perhaps it can change shape like the mimic octopus does, to fool its prey: one moment flat like a ray, the other spiky as a lionfish. But it does not seem to need to be in the sea as an octopus would; it retains its "shape" outside of the water. In any case, I'm too spooked to sleep upstairs, imagining seeing it flattened in the bathtub or landing across my face in the night like a damp hand or eating Wotsit from the inside out. In the morning I will be brave and put my hand inside the driftwood again. In the morning, one day on from the great storm, things will look different. I will sit up now while the candles I lit burn down, looking out to the dark sea.

Morgan wakes on the sofa, the journal open over his torso. He drifted off reading it, away into weird dreams of jellyfish and bees spinning around in the vortex of a storm. It is already bright outside, hazy with heat. He tries to wake up, splashing his face in the kitchen sink, drinking a mug of water and setting the coffee pot up on the gas ring again. He flicks open the journal. His mother was sane; he'd never known her to suffer any kind of delusion. She wasn't flaky or prone to wild imaginings. Her paintings were always from life – mostly the changing landscape of the Headland, or the lake at the nature reserve, the odd object of interest, or wildlife: a blue swift or bright-red fox. He looks back over her description of learning to perceive the creature, how she compares it to what he'd call a Magic Eye picture, one that resolves into three dimensions if you unfocus your eyes. There was a craze for them when he was at primary school, kids spending their playtime passing them around. Has she written this to entertain him? A flight of fancy as she died, high on painkillers when the cancer symptoms became intolerable, making the journal look old, giving him a document to pore over with his historian's mind? Or is it authentic and was she so terribly lonely before he was born that she conjured this story to keep her company? What he knows is that it doesn't add up; fakery was not part of his mother's character. If she experienced it, it was real.

The water creaks in the pipes as Morgan runs a bath. He's out of the door early, journal in his back pocket, striding towards Café Ferdinand. On the way he watches the land-scape. Though he hasn't walked the beach for a while, the lighthouses, old and new, are familiar to him, and the grubby yellow diggers and the green sea mine he liked to clamber all over as a child, pretending it was still live and about to explode, or that it was an alien ship. This used to be his landscape, and the scent of the breeze returns it to him: briny and fresh with a salt-honey edge. He has spent so much time in the city and it clears the smoky air from his lungs. The catch and return of the waves in their soft, distant roar is like an album he used to listen to on repeat. He stops and crouches down for a moment by a rockpool, its water not yet burned away by the sun. He loved these as a child and often stared into them looking for the movement of tiny, transparent crabs and flickering fish. In this one there is a frond of algae and some broken remnants of shells.

As he straightens up, something about the light makes the water in the pool suddenly appear dark, velvety blue and filled with stars, as if it is reflecting the night sky. But it is morning, bright and cloudless. Morgan takes a step back towards the pool, and it is just an ordinary rockpool filled with the miniature rag and bone of the sea, scraps of things once living. He turns to walk away, glances back and once again he sees the night sky, dark and shining in the pool's surface. His ears ring and his head feels unmoored. He sits for a moment on the shingle and takes deep breaths as the surface of his skin shudders. One of his "episodes". He hasn't had one since he was a teenager, and he hasn't taken medication for years. He had a series of them, beginning when he was a child. Each episode began with vibrations in his limbs, a lightness in his body, a fog of static clouding his vision and a low hum in his ears. The very first had happened on the beach on November the fifth, bonfire night. The stars were clear and burning in the black sky, the bonfire hot at Morgan's back, the big moon chalky above him. It had seemed then that he could touch the Milky Way, swirl it with his fingers. Then it was coming down to meet him, closer and closer like a huge spinning shadow punctured with lights. And then he was lying on the shingle, looking up, his mother lifting him by the armpits, dragging him back to the house as the fireworks started. He still remembers her frantic, breathless voice, "You're okay, baby, you're okay. Let's get you inside." And later, as he sat wrapped in a blanket with a hot chocolate, she had said, "I think it was the excitement maybe. I've never seen you do that before."

But it happened again, and his mother was so worried she demanded tests. The doctors couldn't find anything wrong: no epilepsy or blood pressure problem, no tumours or issues with the inner ear. They diagnosed panic attacks. But the feeling was not unpleasant, and after a rest the world would settle, and Morgan felt refreshed and invigorated. He wasn't an anxious child, and the episodes seemed to be triggered by moments of curiosity and deep thought, not fear. Then nothing, not after he moved away from the Headland. Nothing for decades. He has missed his episodes in a way: their vertiginous thrill and aftershock to the brain. He feels like he's had a jump-start. Something about being here, back at the Headland, has brought this on. He rakes a hand through his hair and stands up. The horizon is now steady, and his legs are strong, so he continues to head up the beach.

Café Ferdinand, now with an American diner theme, full of people in the summer cooling down with milkshakes and lemonade, eating whitebait, burgers and chips. A young waitress greets him at the door dressed in dark blue slacks, with her hair tucked into a visor. "Table for one?" Morgan nods and heads to a booth, realising he's hungry, and orders a coffee. "I'll have a look at the menu." He gazes out of the window at the edge of France, fading in and out of the heat haze on the sea. The sea is calm with a purple tinge. Tourists are heading towards the shore, setting up windbreaks and towels.

"Beautiful out there today," says a rasping voice, "and I bet you're after a bacon butty with egg on the side, young man?"

Morgan looks up into the face of Randy Peterson, his mother's long-time friend. Randy's white hair is piled onto her head, her eyelashes thick with mascara, a grin on her face. Morgan stands to hug her. She smells of vanilla as she always has, but her bones feel frail beneath her clothes. She doesn't wear the uniform of the waiters and waitresses, but a simple blue dress with a name badge sewn on.

"Randy, it's good to see you."

"I'd say *haven't you grown* and all that, but I expect you stopped growing twenty years ago, Morgan, and I've said it every time I've seen you. Poor you, having to indulge an old hag like me."

"Never."

Randy lifts her hand and slips into the booth to sit opposite him, and the waitress comes over. "Be a dear, love, bring me a coffee to go with Morgan's here, and bring him a bacon butty, egg on the side. No charge. You've not become a vegan or anything, Morgan?"

"I tried it for a few weeks. Doesn't work for me, no discipline."

"Ah, I don't believe it."

They sip their coffee in silence for a moment. Randy reaches a hand, heavily decorated in rings, to touch his own bare fingers. "I'm sorry about your mum. We all loved her, you know, and next week, it'll be a beautiful funeral, if ever a funeral can be. Lots of lovely flowers, because she adored that silly garden: dog roses and viper's bugloss, irises, even some fennel. She didn't want it too conventional. There are some people coming up, for the procession on the beach. It's still traditional here on the Headland to take the ashes out at night, send some lanterns up. I hope that's okay with you."

It made sense for his mother to be cremated, and to want her ashes scattered at sea on this coast. Morgan couldn't help entertaining the morbid thought that they might blow back in, the burnt dusty pieces of his mother, to mingle with the sand and be patted into sandcastles by children or grit up peoples' ice creams and fish and chips and end up in their teeth.

"You alright, Morgan?"

"Yes, fine, Randy. It's just…surreal I guess, that she'll soon be out at sea, just drifting, just gone."

"None of us are really ever gone, you know. Only our bodies."

This feels faintly religious to Morgan, so he doesn't say anything more. His phone flashes again, and Randy raises her eyebrows, but he just turns it over on the table. The bacon butty arrives, and he sinks his teeth into its slippery grease.

He spends the afternoon in the house, tidying and reading the journal. As the sun goes down, Watchbell becomes lonely, so he walks up the dusky beach to the Hope and Anchor, the seakale tufts of shadow moving in the breeze, the waves shushing out and growling back. The pub is filled with yellow light and rowdy chatter. Lots of people are outside on the terrace in the heat. He takes his pint in its sweating glass and leans over the balustrade, watching the moon reflected on the sea. One group of people have taken all of the outside chairs to cram around their table. They are deep in serious conversation, listening to a wiry, broad-shouldered man who lets his pint of Guinness drip down his arm as he raises it mid-sentence. A woman in the group eyes Morgan between sips of her red wine. She's blonde, with the sharp-lined beauty of someone who doesn't need makeup. Her black top is ribbed cotton with three little buttons. She inclines her head and raises an eyebrow in invitation. One of her friends offers Morgan his chair.

"I'm going for another pint anyway," he says, scraping it back.

"Oh, thanks," says Morgan. It would be rude now not to sit down.

"I'm Ashlie," the woman says, offering her hand. He takes it lightly. Her fingers are cool.

"Morgan."

"Haven't seen you here before." She lights an old-fashioned cigarette and puffs the smoke across his face. It's a pleasant sensation, though it ought not to be.

"I'm here for my mother's funeral. But I used to live here, for a bit. And come here in the summers."

"Sorry to hear about your mother. So, you are sort of a local…" She stretches her arm along the table and her eyes look heavy-lidded for a moment. Their conversation is muted and soft because the man who dominates the group is still talking. He sips from his Guinness again and his gaze falls on them.

"Ash, who's your friend?"

"His name's Morgan," she says. "He's a local."

"Well, not really," Morgan mumbles into his glass.

"I could ask you a few questions then," says the man, who doesn't introduce himself. He has a posh, clipped voice laced with drink, and another accent from elsewhere that rises up from time to time. Morgan cannot place it.

Morgan nods. *Sure. Whatever.* These people seem organised and socially connected, but with an edge to them, so he assumes they are protesting about the closure of the nuclear plant. He doesn't know what he thinks: clean energy but with the threat of catastrophe. What a choice. But he is wrong: that's not why they are here.

"How do you feel, Morgan," says the man, "about this beautiful beach being polluted?"

"I'm not sure what you mean."

"Polluted by people who don't belong on our shores. Coming here. Coming in boats and rocking up here. Quite regularly, they do it."

Morgan feels the heat draining out of his face. These people are not who he thought they were. He's often talked to Maggie about this, and she always leaves the flat to walk off the argument, pacing the city streets. She thinks he's a hypocrite, not socially minded, cruel. She called him a bastard once, which was a poor choice of word. But he's not sure whose side he's on. He tries to be honest with her. He feels protective of his space, suspicious of outsiders. Like everyone, he worries what they may bring, what they might take. But now, seeing the hate in this man's wide blue eyes, his face reddened with drink, he doesn't want to be here, doesn't want to debate the issue. He glances briefly at the moon again, metallic in the sky. He feels lightheaded and fears another episode.

"I don't know," he says. "I can see it's very risky for them to cross the water. Foolish even. And then it's difficult to manage…"

"And they bring their diseases, that's something you can't even see, can't even know…" interrupts one of the group.

"We all know," says Morgan softly, "disease knows no boundaries. I doubt very much…"

"Look," says the leader, gargling slightly, "you can't accept it's okay. This is unspoilt coastline. And then what? Using the health service. Demanding money to live. Children."

"Well, I don't know. I can see where you're coming from, but they must be desperate anyway."

The man waves his hand in dismissal and turns to talk to the others. Morgan isn't of interest now.

"It's a shame," drawls Ashlie, stubbing out her cigarette into a slice of lime. "You could have joined us. I have a feeling something big is going to go down."

"I couldn't really. I have to see to the funeral, then I'm back to the city." He looks into his now empty glass. Ashlie circles his forearm with her cool fingers.

"See you around," she says.

Morgan pushes his chair back and walks until the lights of the Hope and Anchor are at his back, and he is deep in the shadows of the beach.

He lies in his mother's bed in Watchbell House, flat on his back, staring at the ceiling, drifting between sleep and wakefulness. He hears the sea pulling and pushing at the shore, drawing backwards and forwards towards the French coast. What would it be like to board a dinghy and go out onto the blue-black waves? To hope you don't capsize? To cram in shoulder to shoulder, soaked through to the skin? Why would anyone do that? To not be able to see the beach ahead of you in the darkness. To hope it is there and that you'll make it. The room tilts and Morgan slides away into sleep, the sound of the waves coming closer and closer, as if they might pour through the windows of his mother's house and over his head.

<u>Saturday 17th October 1987, 4.05 p.m.</u>

I woke on the sofa this morning, just as the sun was coming up and the blue was draining from the sky. The events of the previous day came into focus: the raging storm, the driftwood, Irene's death, the creature both here and not here seemed the remnants of a weird nightmare. I have them sometimes – bad dreams: hairless mice that I should have looked after trying to escape through holes in Watchbell's skirting boards, things bubbling under the skin of my torso, or the sea seeping through the door. But no, the driftwood was there on the table, Wotsit was draped over my feet, and the crack was still in the windowpane. And what's more, there was an inky glow coming from the hole in the driftwood, and a clicking sound, and the faint smell of smoked lemons. I tugged the blanket off me and felt the chill in the air. I needed to make up a fire. The light inside the hole flickered and then faded. I eyed the driftwood but went first to the kitchenette and filled the kettle. Wotsit stayed curled in the blanket. The glow inside the wood died away as the sun rose; so maybe it only does this in poor light. I knew it was still there. I knew, as I sipped sugary coffee, that if I looked inside the diorama again with one eye closed, I would see it there. My heart pulsed again. Was it dangerous? Could it poison me like a deadly spider? It does have some spidery ways. I suppose I don't care if it's not too painful a death. But I worried for Wotsit.

I rolled up the sleeves of my jumper and approached. Before I could look inside, it oozed out as it had before, and hovered over the table, its many-limbs twisting and coiling, its heart-shaped face with its inky stain, and its iridescent, translucent skin catching the light of the new day from the window behind it. It was easier to see today at first. I think I am getting better at perceiving it. It gave off this faint clicking sound that reminded me of my mother's knitting needles. I didn't know how quickly it would move, what it wanted, or what it would do. I thought about calling a vet, or maybe some specialist in tropical animals, but somehow, I know that's not what this is. And despite my fear, there is this feeling inside me that I don't want to share it. Not yet. I thought it might be thirsty or hungry, so I kept my eyes on it and took a saucer from the cupboard. When I turned on the tap it quivered and disappeared for a second as the water gushed onto the metal, but I knew it was still there and it wobbled back into my vision. I slid the saucer onto the table in front of it. As I moved close, I felt a warmth emanating from the creature. It's a few degrees hotter than me, I'd guess. Hot as a radiator or a bath, maybe slightly too hot to touch but not hot enough to burn. The proboscis came out again then and touched the back of my hand like a thin, silk tongue. Its touch no longer repelled me but felt like a strange form of comfort. Then it moved across to the dish of water. Then the water was gone, as if it had never been, and the dish bone dry. I filled the dish again, and it touched my skin again, and the water vanished again. It was as if the water had vaporized, but there was no steam. All the while the stain on its face moved and rolled like a tiny murmuration of starlings. I wondered if it might eat, but it would touch nothing I tried. Muesli. Cat food. Bread. I presented a slice of apple and the proboscis dabbed over it, but it remained intact on the dish.

After a while, the outline of the creature became harder to see. I can't be sure if my eyes were growing tired and losing their ability to perceive it, or the creature was growing tired and losing its ability to manifest itself to me. I was struck, suddenly, with a desire to capture its image. I felt the possibility of losing it, or my ability to see it, at any moment. Like a memory you think you can never lose, say the face of someone you loved; you think you'll never forget but in fact the image drains of colour and detail like a photo pinned on a sunny wall. I dug about for Adrian's old SLR. I realised it was upstairs and I ran up two steps at a time, heart thrumming. But the creature was still there when I got back, hovering. It seemed in no hurry at all. I didn't use the flash, but still its outline seemed to waver as the shutter clicked. And I will have to get the photos developed. So that's a problem; I can't ask Adrian, I can't send it off – what will anyone developing and printing it make of it? Would they even look at the photos, would they notice, would a photo even come out? I don't know if the way I "see" the creature is how it actually appears. But it is a risk.

So, instead, it seemed I must pick up my brushes and my paints for the first time in a long time. There were dry brushes on the window ledge. I did not want to touch them. I am a painter, yet I have felt for a year that I could never pick up a brush again. You understand this – I know you do. But I told myself this situation was an exception. I just needed to add water. I just needed one or two colours to sketch, to capture an impression to try and explain the existence of this creature to my eye and to my brain. I took my pad from the pantry, where it was wedged behind the step ladder. I opened it at the table in front of the creature. I brought over a pot of water. The water disappeared. I realised the creature was going to keep "drinking" any water I put out, so I wet the brush at the sink instead, carefully sat down in front of the creature, noting its clicking sound had settled now to the soft shushing I had heard last night. I had to close one eye again to perceive its form, to let my vision blur out of focus and I tried, with a dab of the brush into the dried-out indigo, to paint its shape.

But I realised there was something wrong with my seeing. Where I thought I knew a line of its face, and understood where it was, it shifted even as I looked at it. I don't mean it moved; I mean that its shapes would not stay as they were. I knew the tentacles or legs would be hard to capture as they pulsed and crept and flickered, but I had thought I could sketch its heart-shaped "face". It was like this, yes, but also now a clover leaf, then a pansy with its four sections and its stained centre. Then it was cat-like, moth-like, almost amphibian and somewhat human. The stain at its centre transformed all the time like a storm cloud and sometimes I could grasp nothing.

When I paint the sea, it moves, and when I paint the sky, broad and ever-changing: I can look up from the easel and find the clouds have shattered and reformed. I suppose it was a problem like that, but with a living being. But this was also the first time I had broken my creative block over trying to paint. I thought of the unfinished paintings upstairs, the oil canvases with their potato-scented paint taking months to truly dry, the watercolours dry as dead leaves and half-blank. This was a kind of progress.

What I did not bank on was the creature, slyly, as I worked my lines, reaching out its proboscis again and dipping it into my palette. It chose Mars Violet 411, but it was a little mixed with the indigo. I thought maybe it was eating it and wondered if it might not be good for it. The proboscis drew the colour in, and I felt the creature vibrate, just a little, through the humming of the tabletop. Wotsit woke up suddenly and darted under the sofa, so I drew back, retreating to where the fridge stood, thinking perhaps some terrible thing was about to happen. But what happened was this: the stain, which I had seen as mostly grey or green-gold like my eye, or ginger like Wotsit, was suddenly suffused with purple, and it had grown, as though a drop of purple was spreading out in water. It seemed to be using the colour to make the stain larger and more vibrant, and now I could see it better than before, the whole of it. I smiled, ear to ear, almost laughed, and felt the strangeness of those deep muscles in my face, coming back to life.

It was then that the knock on the door came, and I panicked.

The phone rings again, this time sounding across the beach because Morgan has taken it off silent. The display flashes *Maggie: Night Out*; he's never changed it: she's still a one-night stand.

"Hi, Maggie." He folds the page of the journal over and places it next to him on the shingle.

"Morgan, are you alright? I've been phoning…"

"Yeah, sorry, Mags; it's been pretty full-on here, organising everything, you know."

Her voice softens, "Morgan, I'm sorry, I just wanted to make sure you arrived okay; you were going to text? But you've got a lot on your mind. Was the house okay?"

Morgan closes his eyes against the sun, high now, reaching its peak.

"It's fine. I'm just going through her stuff. There isn't much of it, but the canvasses – I'm not sure what to do with those."

"Oh, I'd love to see those," breathes Maggie.

"How are you doing then? All okay in the city?"

"Okay. Baby's very lively, kicking away in there. I think he wants out. He or she. There was a moment the other day I thought you would've found cool: he was moving about under there like the Loch Ness monster…It's so hot here though, Morgan. I wish I was on the coast with you.

I've been going to work just for the air-con." She laughs. "Anyway, I'm blathering on."

Maggie speaks to him from a city that now seems so far away, trying to reach him. He fails to hear the need in her voice, the mother in her trying to emerge.

"No, Maggie, tell me. How's the work going?" Morgan wants to hear her talk about anything but the baby undulating in her belly. If they don't talk about it, he can pretend it doesn't exist. He can pretend he is not going to let her down.

"Well, writing up the latest stuff. Reading a lot about quantum time. I can't do much in the lab at the moment as it's not safe. But it's mind-bending, Morgan, the fact that we only perceive time the way we do, as a straight line, past to future, because...because we don't see things in enough detail...Ah, I'm not explaining it well..."

This again. The slice in the donut. Time feels real enough to him. His mother's death is in his past. Morgan is half-listening, watching the white clapboard cottage to his right. It's an old fisherman's house with a wooden sign above the door: Squid Studio & Gallery. The door is open, and he can see a woman inside the cool, pale space. A rusted anchor and a pile of turquoise crab nets decorate the garden, hydrangeas and white roses growing around them. Something about it is familiar, but he's never heard of the studio.

"Listen, Maggie, I'm really glad you're okay. Try to stay cool; I know it must be hot there. The funeral is in a couple of days, and then I'll be home. There's nothing much I can do here after that."

"It's okay, Morgan. Take your time. It's important. And anyway, first babies are always late, aren't they? I've got a few weeks. I'm only sorry I can't be there with you."

Morgan feels a pang of guilt that he's relieved Maggie can't be here.

"What was that about quantum time?"

Maggie laughs again, a girlish giggle from the smart scientist. "I'll draw you a diagram when I see you, Morgan."

"You're too clever for me, Maggie, that's the real trouble."

"Oh no, that's not the trouble. It's that none of us is quite clever enough…I love you, Morgan."

He isn't sure if he's ever heard Maggie say this, or not in this way anyway. His face flashes hot, then cold as if the temperature has suddenly dropped.

"I'll see you soon, Maggie. Bye now."

He slides the phone off and runs a hand down his unshaven jaw. He is almost certain now he's out of the city and has some distance from Maggie that he must tell her: he can't be a father. He didn't have one, does not have one and does not know how to be one. Maggie and the baby will be better off without him in their lives. After the funeral he'll work out how to tell her.

He wanders back to Watchbell House and the cool shade of the living room, journal in his hand.

The knocking became insistent, and with each knock the outline of the creature trembled and then disappeared, until I could see only a cloud of purple drifting in the air. I heard Adrian's voice on the outside of the yellow door. The scene was something like this:

"Dolores, it's me. Are you there?" Whilst he'd hammered with his fist, his voice was tentative and soft. I hadn't seen him for months, and here he was at the door of Watchbell House. I let him in.

"Hi," I said.

"Hi." He smiled, his arm resting on the doorframe. He's always had this slightly lopsided smile from a harelip corrected as a child. He looked well, his sandy hair growing out, designer stubble, a smart jumper.

"Can I come in?"

I glanced behind me. Nothing but Wotsit sitting upright on the kitchen chair, staring at an almost-blank space in front of him, a fizz of imperceptible purple, like dust motes in the light. I looked terrible, I realised, wearing one of Adrian's old, too-big woolly jumpers, my hair unwashed, no make-up. Adrian went to the kettle and put it on to boil.

"Are you okay?"

I told him I was but that there was no power. He said the radio mast was being fixed and I should at least get radio soon.

"But you don't have to stay here, Dol."

Wotsit jumped down and weaved around Adrian's legs, and Adrian lifted him up and kneaded his big fingers into his ginger fur. Cat bliss. I suppose we had both missed him. But he has not touched me for the longest time. He used to brush the back of my neck just so and I knew what he wanted, and I wanted it too. I loved the warm weight of him pressed into me, making me feel I could never drift away.

"I'm okay here," I told him.

"Look," he said, "this is just a studio, a beach hut. I worry about you here on your own."

"It's hardly that," I said. "It's been standing here for a hundred years. The fishermen were safe here and it was good enough for them. The storm last night hardly touched it."

"But it's cold and small. In the middle of nowhere." He hugged Wotsit closer and kissed the top of his head.

I couldn't agree. We had always disagreed about this. I told him I just needed to build the fire, that was all, and I started to do so, feeling stupid because I couldn't get the kindling to catch. He was always the one that started the fire, while I got some dinner going on the stove, or ran a bath after a day getting sunburnt in the garden. Crouched down with the newspaper and matches, I just kept telling him things work for me here, it's beautiful, the school is only around the corner.

"But it's not a place to live. It was only for summer and weekends, Dolores. No-one lives here year-round."

But he's wrong. Irene retired here and lived here all year. But I didn't say anything about her because she's gone now, scooped out of her life by the storm.

"Solomon and Seb, and Randy, they all live here."

"But that's different."

"My work's only up the road, in town."

He sighed and made us coffee, filling the cups too high and forgetting my sugar.

"Why not get yourself a flat in town then? A proper, warm place and you can walk to work. We can just sell this or rent it out in the season, that would pay well. And you can still come here to paint or for the beach."

The kindling lit then, and I got the fire going and it gave me a reason to hide my sulk. I didn't ever want to sell Watchbell or share it with others. I love its black walls and its floorboards and its yellow window frames. I love more than anything its unfenced garden of salvage and seakale and wild poppy and gorse with the square power station glowing in the background. I love the changing sky and the shingle and the bleak, blown sea, the dandelions melting away and the smooth stones and the lonely lighthouse. The sparse disorder. We had come here every summer and sometimes on the weekend after seeing it for sale on an impromptu beachcombing trip. I would paint and Adrian would run or swim. We'd visit the town for tea and cake and go out to the castle. It was a break from the city for him, and we lived close enough to keep an eye on it. He was right: I wasn't meant to live here. But we are not those people anymore and he's now in the city where he works, and I can stay here, be here forever if I want to.

"Dol, I don't want you to put your life on hold."

"I'm not. I'm teaching. I'm okay."

"Are you painting?" He saw my watercolours on the table, the beginnings of my odd sketch. I told him yes, I was just trying my hand at a still life.

"That's a beautiful bit of driftwood." His hand went out.

Suddenly I burned with rage; it came from nowhere.

"Don't touch it!" I hissed, and he drew his hand in.

"Are you alright?"

"Look, I think you should go." I found myself saying this, but I don't think I wanted him to go. He looked at me then, long and hard, and put Wotsit down. Wotsit came to the fire, which had now started to warm the room. It crackled with its woody scent. I realised Adrian had driven for an hour or more to get here, perhaps contending with fallen trees and redirected traffic. I should have been offering for him to stay. He had been worried with no way of contacting me out here on this exposed coast. But I had not worried about him at all. I wonder if that means I don't care about him anymore, or even that I am a terrible person with a "cold heart". Is that what people mean when they say that? We spoke like strangers, awkwardly, when actually, now he was here, I longed for him to reach his arms around and draw me in. What happened, happened to us both, but we have been changed by it in such different ways, we are now alien to each other.

I think of him as being from a past existence and living now in a new reality: a flat in the city, a classy, sophisticated life. Perhaps he has a new girlfriend. And he has always loved his job as a broker, so maybe it's best this way. I backtracked and said that I was sorry and tried to persuade him to stay.

"I've got tinned spaghetti. Surely that can entice you?"

A slight smile, but I had already offended him.

"I know your painting is important. I know you like this place, Dolores, but you can't stay here forever. You have to come back to the real world."

"Is the city the real world?"

"Not necessarily, but reality I mean. Life goes on."

"I am living, Adrian. Just not with you."

I didn't add that this was what *he* had wanted. Everything I said started to sound cruel, but I felt he was being cruel to me too. He had come to check on me, but also to persuade me to leave this beautiful and bleak place. I knew then that he did not understand Watchbell House and why I will never give it up. I knew I couldn't possibly tell him about the creature either. It must stay my secret, at least for now. Adrian soon left, closing the cottage door carefully behind him, crunching back up the shingle to his car.

17th October 1987. Late.

After Adrian left, I sat by the fire and watched the driftwood for signs of life. While he was here, I half wanted the creature to come out so I could show him, share it with him. Perhaps he would know what to do. We used to solve all our problems together, believing that nothing could conquer us. That was a big part of what our love was about. But then I was relieved when he left, and the creature was still my secret. The fire blazed hot in the wood burner and Wotsit fell asleep. I leafed through the Yellow Pages, wondering if I could call someone, and who I should call. Pest control? Definitely not. The local zoo? The aquarium? It didn't seem to need to live in water, even if it drank a lot. I assumed that the driftwood had come from the sea, so the creature had too, but I could be wrong. What if it found the driftwood on the shore and went inside? Perhaps it was a new species, an escaped species, or something washed up from a boat from another country? I will go to the library next week, if it is still open after the storm, and try to figure it out. They will have a better encyclopaedia there. But I know, somehow, because of the way the creature is so difficult to perceive, that it is not of this world. And who would I call for that?

I put some coal on top of the wood so that the fire would burn steadily. I dozed off with the Yellow Pages on my lap. And then I felt a tugging on the book and opened one eye to see the creature there. It hovered like a hummingbird, using its vibrating limbs to stay in the air, and the purple stain shone, fluxing. It had quite a grip on the opened page and I saw it had punctured the paper as if taking a series of small bites. Paper. So perhaps it liked to eat paper? I tried it with some old newspapers from the kindling basket, and again it punched some tiny holes, like Morse code, into it. Then it seemed drawn to the fire and hovered there, the flames reflecting on its translucent surface making the whole of it easier to see. I worried it was getting too close, but it hummed and clicked as if satisfied or happy, and Wotsit opened one eye but did not seem to be worried by the creature. As I watched, the stain resolved into a set of new shapes, defined, thin and made of lines and loops. I realised they were letters and numbers. Fragments of text. They made no sense at first, but it dawned on me that they had come from the pages the creature had eaten. I laughed, softly so as not to startle. It seems the creature absorbs shapes and images and they flash upon the screen of its face. I can't work out if it is trying to communicate, or if this is a by-product of its "eating" of the paint and paper. It hovered a while longer by the fire, then shot, like a jet of water, back to its driftwood home. There it remained for the rest of the day, the only sign of its existence the heat coming from the wood and a faint shushing sound. I looked at my watercolour sketch. I saw face, flower, insect, fish – nothing that made any sense. It is the strangest painting I have ever made. I was reminded of the pansies growing in Watchbell's garden, of storm clouds, human features, felines and the mandibles of a bee.

I have decided to give the creature a name. Because of its resemblance to a violet flower with its segmented, stained face, and its choice of Mars Violet 411 from my water-colour box, I will call it "Violet 411", or "Violet" for short. I doubt if it really is either male or female, but I will think of it as "she" because Wotsit is a "he" and that will balance my little family. I'm tired now and will sleep on the sofa again, just to be near her, just in case she needs anything.

Morgan is pulling out every drawer in the kitchen; that roll of film from the old SLR camera could still be in Watchbell House. His mother had a "messy drawer" full of spare batteries; clothes pegs and safety pins; Sellotape and string and gummed-up tubes of glue. He feels around in the shoebox again, but there is nothing in there but the fragile newspaper clippings. He sits on the sofa, head in hands, trying to think. There is a photo, at least one. There are sketches. Where would they be? Who is Adrian? Why did his mother never mention him? She never mentioned anyone. He goes up to the bedroom, canvasses stacked up against the wall where she left them, ready for Morgan to collect. He leafs gently through them but none of them show anything resembling the creature she describes, and they are finished pieces, in some cases framed, not sketches. He lies down on the bed and stares at the cracks in the ceiling. When he was little, and they spent summers here, they shared Watchbell's one bed. He wasn't allowed to sleep next to his mother in the flat; he had his own room with boxes of Lego, and soft toys lined up at the foot of the bed. When he woke up in the night, really scared from a dream, he had to stay in his own bed, but she would come and be next to him, lying on the floor, until he fell asleep again. But at Watchbell, they tucked under the covers together and he slept resting against his mum's warm back, listening to her breathe in the dark. He reaches beside him now to the nightstand and pulls out the little drawer. Without looking, he feels inside. His fingers catch a small plastic cylinder. He lifts it out and holds it up: a roll of Kodak film, spooled back in, never developed.

It is late afternoon and the beach is busy, groups of people strolling, or sitting on the shingle with cans of drink, a few brave souls in the chilly sea. Morgan ventures to the door of Squid Studio and Gallery and knocks gently. The door is propped open. Nobody replies, so he walks in. On every wall: a striking drawing of the local landscape, stylised and stark, each image made only of light and shadow, the ink brown-black. There is one of the old lighthouse, rising darkly from the flat beach, which catches his eye.

"That one is three hundred. Limited edition print. Original goes for six."

He turns to see a woman in her mid-fifties wearing a long blue tunic, wild dark curls cut around her ears, broad shoulders on a petite frame. She smiles, then laughs.

"Just doing my hard sell…Feel free to look around. I work a lot in squid ink, hence the name of the studio." She frowns at him for a moment, then sits behind a desk fashioned from driftwood and opens her laptop. She sighs and blows a stray curl from her eyes. Morgan looks at the drawings on display: landscapes, but also exquisite images of shells and barnacles, the intricacies of the spiked sea mine, washed up seaweed pods and empty crab shells – the gorgeous detritus of the Headland. Then sketches of wrecked boats and grubby digging equipment. There is no turning away, no prettifying in these pictures; they are bold and raw.

"Wait a minute…Are you…isn't it…Morgan?" she says and half rises from her seat.

"Yes…I…"

"Claire. Claire Marston. I used to babysit for you sometimes, in the summers. When I was back from art school, god, years ago before my master's degree."

"Oh my god, yes you did!"

Morgan flushes, remembering snippets of Claire cooking him spaghetti hoops; drawing together on big pieces of paper spread out in the living room of Watchbell House; persuading her to let him stay up late to watch movies. Claire comes from behind the desk and hugs him.

"So sorry, Morgan, about your mum. She was great. You know she taught me so much of this –" she waves a hand around the gallery – "I owe her a lot for inspiring me, making sure I got into art school."

"That's amazing. She must have been proud to see these. I love them. I think Mum and I have the same taste."

She smiles and squeezes his shoulder, but her smile fades as her gaze shifts past Morgan's face and out of the window. He turns to look at them: a small group, framed in the white wood, kicking stones on the beach.

"Bloody right-wingers," says Claire. "Always find some pretext to be here in the summer."

"What do you mean? What for?"

"Oh, the usual crap. So close to France we get refugees sometimes coming in on boats, often from Iran originally. So bloody dangerous, but we always help them. They underestimate the waves, and what to do when they get in. A couple of times a year we're out there with blankets and tea before the police arrive. These blokes think it's their job instead to protect the border from a handful of desperate people; they've been known to try to put them back in the sea. Then they also hate artists, or people like Randy because they think she's "queer" or whatever. Their idea of a holiday: spoiling for a fight; always getting into a scuffle in the local pubs. Lately they've been getting worse, and more of them seem to gather."

"They don't have a point about that?" ventures Morgan, peering at the group through the window. "I mean, it's illegal and it's so dangerous for everyone."

Ashlie, the woman he sat with at the pub, is among the group. He ducks further into the studio so she can't see him.

Claire looks at him sharply. "They're desperate, Morgan. If you knew what they came from…"

She sighs and sits down at the desk again. "But it's so good to see you, Morgan. Look at you, fucking tall, aren't you? Don't get that from your mum."

"Not sure who I get it from."

Claire is quiet for a moment. Then she says, "My mum and dad broke up. I was a baby. Dad was here though; this was his house at one stage. He let me have it for my studio. Fisherman, third generation. He'll be down for the funeral actually. I think you'll remember my dad, Solomon. He liked playing with you when he came back in the summers. When you were a kid."

Morgan remembers only vaguely a tall, dark-haired man with wiry arms swinging him up under the cold crest of a wave. There are more memories there, slowly emerging like sunbeams from behind thick cloud, but Claire interrupts his thoughts:

"It's not easy though, even when both parents are nearby. Everyone wants their folks to be together, to believe in love and all that. I'm still with my hubby, though occasionally I want to stab him with a breadknife. But we're together mostly for my boy, my gorgeous son Arthur. I wanted us both there for him. Of course, he's at uni now. Marine biology! And me and his dad, we sort of got used to each other over the years." She gives a soft smile that suggests she is more than used to him.

Morgan smiles back and gazes out at the group on the beach, wondering why they'd come just to stir up trouble. Sometimes other people's generosity is unbearable, perhaps. Or there is the idea that you own your land, and nobody else may ever set foot on it. It's crowded enough. It's teeming with threat.

"Claire, I wonder if you can help me with something? I found an old roll of camera film amongst Mum's stuff.

Do you know anyone who can develop it? I'm curious, I guess, to see if there is anything on there."

Claire takes the film from him and turns it in her palms. "Don't see these much anymore. I know someone with a dark room, old uni friend. I can get it printed in a couple of days, if there is anything to print. Sometimes the light gets into them, turns the film black. Picture's still there I guess, but stained with darkness, too dark to see."

"Yes," Morgan says, "I realise that might be a possibility."

<u>Sunday 18th October 1987, 5.25 p.m.</u>

On Sundays I visit my mother at *The Lilacs*. I wasn't sure if I would manage to this week, not knowing if the buses would run. But I was worried about her. It meant leaving Violet and Wotsit alone in Watchbell House. In the morning, Violet oozed out of the driftwood, a cloud of purple moving across her face, her weird limbs creeping and vanishing as she rolled across the kitchen counter. Her proboscis settled on the label of the marmalade jar, and once she had felt all over it, the print faded as if it had been left out in the sun. I had lain awake all night on the sofa, feeling bad about Adrian, listening to her shushing sounds, feeling her low vibrations through the driftwood. The power station was lit with an eerie glow, but other than that, blackness everywhere, still no electricity here. I kept wondering if Violet needed anything, if she was cold or hungry. I am still worried that she doesn't have what she needs to survive. I made a strong, sugary coffee and she stretched her body like a sparkling skin around the coffee cup, turning it lukewarm in moments. The sun, rising in the windows, reflected on her, was a greenish yellow. She brushed my skin where I held my cup and all of the hairs rose on my arm.

"You like it warm, don't you?" I ventured, thinking it right to talk to her. Wotsit pricked up his ears and meandered over. Violet's stain diffused over all of her being, just for a moment, and I felt myself flush, as if found out, but for what I couldn't say. I left her a number of bowls of water on every available surface, and scraps of paper where I thought she could reach them, ripping up old romance paperbacks and glossy magazines. Wotsit had his food bowl as always, and anyway will come and go as he pleases. He disappeared for three days once and came back with half a dead vole clamped in his jaws, his expression somewhere between tenderness and murderous intent. Instinct is such an odd thing. I left them there, so afraid that one would devour the other, but needing to see my mother. Care is impossible to distribute or divide, just like love. Sometimes you have to take a risk, I suppose. I imagined all kinds of horrors could meet me on my return.

There are fewer buses on Sundays, but always one at 10.08. It was there, in defiance of the fallen tree at the side of the road: an empty number 20 bus.

"I wondered if anyone would come," said the driver as I made my way on. I watched the sea as we went along the coast, my own black house standing on the shingle. We swung away from the narrow-gauge railway line, away from the shore and towards the town. Most of the houses near the coast are one storey, perhaps with a dormer. Most looked intact, their manicured roses a little frayed, their rendered walls a little muddy. But one had an oak lying embedded in its roof, its roots lifting the tarmac off the road. Another roof was shattered to expose its wooden beams.

My mother has been at *The Lilacs* for six years. At first it was little things: forgetting what she'd gone into a room for, a favourite film star's name. Getting ready at three a.m. and waiting in the dark in her best clothes for a date with me to have afternoon tea. But then the rooms themselves became unfamiliar. She couldn't find her bedroom in the house she'd lived in for years. Dad died in 1971, summertime, clutching his chest at a family picnic; but she started to ask when he was coming home from work. Sometimes when I visit, she knows me. Sometimes she doesn't.

The lilacs that line the path to the Victorian home were bedraggled, themselves like elderly folk trying to stand upright, still beautiful but diminished. There was a spit of drizzle in the air, the wind blustering and silver clouds spinning above my head. They know me well at the home and buzzed me through. The receptionist has this glossy helmet of hair; she's kind but does not look it. I asked if everything was okay. "Luckily," she said. "I thought the roof was going to come in, but we only lost a few tiles in the end. She's in the garden room."

There were a few people there, nodding on their chairs. A woman knitting a long yellow scarf smiled up at me as I passed by. Click, click, clack. My mother knitted too, sometimes, but I saw her half-finished sweater was resting on a side table and not in her hands today. Mum was facing the garden, which was strewn with leaves and bruised apples. She sat upright with her back to me. Low sunlight illuminated the wisps of hair at her neck. The sight of the soft, back-lit skin of her ears made me pause before I went around to her and knelt down. She held out her hand, knotted with blue veins, her wedding ring spinning on her finger. My mother who used to scoop me up when I fell from my bike. Who kissed my forehead as I fell asleep. She looked up. Today, she knew it was me.

"Dolores. Dolly-mixture mine." She is the kindest woman I know. She would do anything for me, though now she can't do much at all. My sister, living in Seattle, never visits. Busy with her four children and her big house. My mother thinks she lives there because she likes the rain. But it's because love is too painful to face at all sometimes. She had adored our big, jovial, expansive father and found herself a big, jovial, expansive husband. Her love for our mother was deep though, and as soon as her memory began to fail, Cassie couldn't accept it and was gone. Out of sight, out of mind. Mum told me to sit down.

"You look pale, did something happen?" I hesitated, then told her about the storm.

"Terrible business," she sighed, and then smoothed her skirt. "Living near the coast we are so exposed. That ridiculous Fish man, saying that everything was alright. Some men think they know everything. Your father, he always said, 'Just one more cigarette; I'll give up after Christmas. I'll give up after the summer holiday.' It gave him up instead."

I winced. When she was lucid like this, she was also bitter about Dad. We looked at the garden in silence for a while. When I was a toddler, she unzipped a pod growing in the garden, to show me the runner beans inside. I still remember my astonishment. She would shine an apple on her cardigan before she gave it to me. Dead-headed the roses in autumn. Lifted a rabbit from its hutch, catching its rangy legs so I could stroke it. Its eyes shone and its whole being quivered.

Out of nowhere she said, "Dolly – the only way to get over sadness is to let it be part of you." Her eyes were clear and green, and she gripped my hand. "Let it come through you. Like a wave. Like the wind. It burns cold. You think it will take you with it. But it won't."

I couldn't really listen to this, so I paced over to the serving hatch and asked for a pot of tea. We always have tea. I forgot the cakes today, which I usually get on the local high street, but these are extreme circumstances. The man at the hatch was bald, with a broad, open face. I fumbled with the cups, the pot and the tray. When I got back to her and poured it out, she only said, "Wait for it to brew, before you pour it. And wait for your father – I'm sure he's parched."

When I got home, the walk to Watchbell's door seemed endless. All was quiet and still, save the flutter of the wind. Sometimes there are tourists around on Sundays, leaving their cars on the shingle and beachcombing, riding the little train or going for fish and chips. You would like those things. But autumn is quiet, and I guess the storm has kept everyone away. It felt as though I could be the only living soul on the Headland in that moment. What might that be like? Like being washed up on a shingle island. I would have to learn how to fish, without Solomon to teach me. Maybe I would repair a derelict fishing boat like the ones above the shore. I would have my garden where I could grow potatoes, onions, cabbages. I could paint all day, though I might need to make paints from ground stones and crushed insects and the pollen of roses, from beetroot and rhubarb and poppies. I might catch lizards basking on stones and roast them. A life alone has its appeal, but I wanted only to find Wotsit and Violet had not eaten each other and would be there for me when I opened the door.

Wotsit was curled next to the fire, which had only hot embers from this morning and no flames. His eyes were shut, and his back moved gently up and down. The driftwood was on the table. I could not see Violet and assumed she was inside, but I realised the embers of the fire were purple-tinged, closed one eye and glimpsed her there in the grate. I was unable to move and a feeling as hot as the embers rose in my throat. It was a kind of horror: she had roasted herself. I had let her die. But she quivered, shushing as before, whilst letters and numbers coursed across her face. She was fine, as far as I could tell. She really does like to be warm...As my heart steadied, I saw she was bigger. Scraps of paper littered the room. She had punched holes in it all, rendering the paperbacks plot-less, the adverts confetti. I poured a whisky, my hand shaking.

Morgan has only vague memories of his grandmother, who died when he was still a toddler, but he does remember visiting *The Lilacs*, the smell of gravy, and lavender soap, and the vast, grassy garden out back he was sometimes allowed to play in. She was very frail by then, with papery, lined skin like the pages of an old book, and blue veins bulging in her hands. There was always something knitted for him: a pullover with a train image, or a teddy bear wearing a waistcoat with real buttons. Then one day, they stopped getting the bus to *The Lilacs*.

Morgan lifts the fragile newspaper clippings from the shoebox and sifts them onto the table. They are cut out neatly and ordered, though here and there a punched hole, like something a bookworm or a moth might make, obliterates a word. The first is a big square with the heading **Great Storm Kills 18** cut from *The Times*, dated Saturday, 17th of October 1987. He reads,

"Gale force ***** ripped through the UK in the early hours of Friday morning, leaving devastation in their wake. Eighteen people have lost their lives, hundreds are injured, and many are left without power. There is an estimated 300 million insurance bill, and a number of ancient, protected ***** have been uprooted and destroyed. The Home Secretary, Douglas ****, stated that the death toll may well have been higher if the storm hadn't struck during the night, and cited this as one of the worst disasters to hit our island in recent decades."

There is a faded photograph of an uprooted tree, its huge root facing the camera, almost as large as its bedraggled, leafy crown which hangs over a crushed car, its roof caved in. A man stands improbably on top of the tree, casting his eyes across the street, as if just deposited from the eye of the storm. His life seems miraculous. Morgan reads on, about the clean-up, the amazing escapes – one woman walked all night, in labour, trying to reach the hospital with her husband, climbing over fallen oaks and tangled telephone lines, only to have to turn back to her home and give birth there. A skiff on the Serpentine is photographed resting in a tree, as if it were a sky-boat just taken to mooring there. It is the trees that he thinks about the most. The ancient tulips, oaks and yews in Kew Gardens, lost forever. Now, trees are everywhere. Morgan remembers a few years ago the government declared The Year of the Tree, and began a panic drive to protect and reforest as much as possible. People notice trees these days as they didn't before. They have moved from the background, from lining roads and catching buses with their branches and providing shade in the park, to the foreground. People look at them again. And it seems, in 1987, that people looked at them too. Felled. Invading the byways. Their deadly weight, their awesome power. Their slow time.

There is another clipping here, from the same newspaper, a few days later. **Dow Jones Falls 508 points in Stock Market ***astrophe.** An image of a man with his head in his hands and a phone cradled at his ear accompanies the headline. Morgan has heard about Black Monday, his mother mentioned it a few times. Morgan hadn't connected the storm to the crash, but the article details the power outage stranding the markets for the longest time in recent history, as well as the Silkworm missiles sent by Iran to hit an American supertanker in the Persian Gulf. "Silkworm" seems an odd name for a missile – something so destructive and full of noise and fire.

There is a third clipping, its font different. It must be from another paper, perhaps a local one, and is dated 25th of October 1987. It is from the announcements section:

"Deaths: Irene Marston, 16th of October 1987. Irene was tragically killed in the storm and will be **** to rest after a funeral in St Martin's Church, The ****land, on the 31st of October at 2 p.m. All members of the local ****unity are welcome. At 5 p.m., Irene's ***** will be scattered on the coast which was beloved to her. She is survived by her son, William, and Sebastian and ***omon, her grandchildren."

<u>Saturday 31ˢᵗ October 1987. Night.</u>

Irene's funeral was today. Life has settled into a strange pattern since the storm. A couple of weeks ago the radio crackled into life, and the lights came on, and I listened to the news which was about the stock market. I can't understand it all, but it certainly sounds bad. The song "It's a Sin" keeps playing, and that other one with all its melodrama about dropping breakables. I couldn't help thinking how appropriate these songs are to these past few weeks. Life seems fractured, weird, repetitive. The phone came back a few days after this, and I spoke to Adrian, who's stressed about his job, but said my finances were okay. It's not like I have much to worry about losing. I am back at work, with less time to write this diary. The students were jittery after the storm, like spooked animals. To combat this, I suggested we paint it using water colour, trying to conjure the vivid memories of lightning and high waves, debris in the air. And today, on Halloween, there are pumpkin lanterns glowing in the windows, and Irene was laid to rest.

Violet languishes in the grate, where she likes a low flame. At night, the driftwood glows with her inside and I want to stay on the sofa and be near her, though her "shushing" grows louder, like the sound inside a shell. When she doesn't "shush" she "click-clacks". I've developed a kind of insomnia; I'm wired but exhausted, only sleeping for one or two hours, then waking again. Wotsit doesn't follow me in this; as winter draws close, he slumbers for longer, cosy on the sofa or in front of the fire. He has accepted Violet but is often miffed when the water evaporates from his bowl. I'm almost out of paper, which Violet punches holes in with alacrity. Now the power is back, I feel a shift. I have the sense we are no longer hidden from the world. Violet grows larger and easier for me to see. The stain shifts across her face in letters and numbers and shapes. When she is not "shushing", she vibrates or hums, wrapping herself around anything warm. I sense she will not like the winter, and I must keep the fire lit. I also need to do something about her, though I don't know what. After dinner, which for me is not paper but some tinned food, I talk to her. I can't tell if she listens or not, or even if she has "ears", but she hovers near me, her being shifting and phasing, puncturing a magazine or a book. I tell her about my day, my students, the weather. She doesn't seem to mind, at least.

I left them to go to the funeral, tired and wide awake, my eyeballs shiny in the breeze. St Martin's church. Randy wore a beautiful dress of black crêpe de chine. I have never seen Solomon in a suit before, only coarse fisherman's clothes. He'd combed his mop of curls in an attempt to control it, but it only looked wilder, like a storm cloud. He and Seb and other relatives carried Irene's wicker coffin to the alter. Tony the vicar said his words about ashes and dust. We are all ashes, I thought. All about to dissipate in the wind, our atoms clinging together God knows how. Bob Dylan's "You're Gonna Make Me Lonesome When You Go" played over the tinny speakers. The coffin travelled along a belt and then a velvet curtain closed, as at the end of an amateur play. It rained in the scrubby churchyard. We were to meet later for the scattering of Irene's ashes at sea.

In the meantime, we went to Café Ferdinand, where Randy had put on bacon butties and tea laced with whisky. People talked in low voices about their lucky escapes in the storm. One got out of his car just before a tree crushed it. One who had not gone to bed, staying up late to watch the wind pick up, avoided the lamppost that crashed into his bedroom. They talked of birds wheeling around in the sky; cracking timbers and sliding rooftiles; a pet dog that howled for hours; a rabbit who survived in the pitch dark of her upended hutch. They talked about the power station, thinking of Chernobyl last year, sickly images of those killed still coming to us on TV, and later, images of children born with huge heads or missing limbs. How close were we to that? Seb overheard one of these conversations. He was dark-eyed today, quiet.

"There was no danger. We have a number of safety mechanisms in place." Since last year, he has found it harder when people talk about his job at the plant. He's defensive. Those that were talking stopped and made their excuses to walk away.

"Eat something," Randy told me. "You look peaky." She added more whisky to my tea and a dripping bacon roll to my hand. I bit into it, and it didn't taste like stone as food usually does to me now. It tasted good and I ate it quickly, like a starved animal, and licked my fingers. I caught her watching me as she circulated in the café, a foot taller than anyone, offering refreshment and kind words. She nodded at me. As the light faded, we made a little procession along the beach, some of us with lanterns. The air was damp and cool, the tall black lighthouse and power station at our backs, a constant, glowing presence. Solomon had Irene's ashes, and we watched as he and Seb got into the fishing boat with them, awkward in their suits. We stood at the shore with our lanterns, an audience to the indigo waves that took them out, the lamp on the boat a single smudge of white. I saw their silhouettes, their spider hands casting the ash. It was siphoned up on the breeze like iron filings. It darkened the grey sky for a moment, then it disappeared. Goodbye, Irene – taken by the storm.

Morgan is out walking the beach at night. The sky is still tinged with purple even though it is very late. He breathes in the cool air. The journal is on the oak table by the window back in the house; he doesn't want to read any more tonight. He was hoping to finish reading it before the funeral, but there is so much to take in, so many things he didn't know about his mother's experience of the world, so many questions about the people within its pages. He hopes one could be his father, but the more he reads, the more doubtful he becomes. He doesn't recognise himself in anyone but his mother, and even then, he is so very different from her: more sceptical and more melancholy.

On the coastline, in the distance, a silhouetted group of three are approaching him. Their voices are loud and the shingle crunches under their steps. As they draw level, one stops, halting the other two, and says, "Saw you at the gallery, talking to that woman."

At times like this, Morgan is glad he's so tall, even if he's not broad. Most people have to raise their chin to look at him.

"You know," says another, whose voice is mucousy in his throat, "she helps immigrants, illegals. Positively encourages them."

"I can't say I did know that," says Morgan.

The third man, shorter than the others but with a head like a cannonball, says, "Who are you, anyway? I've seen you in that café, talking to the owner – that guy in drag. And I've seen you somewhere else too."

Morgan winces in the darkness. The sea whispers gently in and out.

"You're not from here," the first man says.

"Are you from the Headland?" Morgan counters, putting one hand in his pocket and looking up the beach to the lights of the oyster bar, estimating its distance at a running pace.

"We come here regular, every summer. We rent the same place." He gestures vaguely up the beach. "So, we may as well be locals."

"I'm here for a funeral," says Morgan, the pores on his skin prickling.

"Ah, condolences for that, mate," says the mucous-voiced man. He takes a step back.

"Who died?" says Cannonball Head. "Anyone we know?"

"My mother."

The three men look at him and he turns on his heel, not waiting for what they might say, and heads back up the shingle to Watchbell House. He turns once, when he's close to the garden, the spiky shadows of the elder bushes marking its boundaries, expecting the men at his back. But they are still in the distance, loitering by the rusty old sea mine, their voices drowned out by the waves.

Friday 6th November 1987. Early.

We always have bonfire night on the beach; it's a Headland tradition. This year there was more than usual to pile onto the bonfire – things broken by the storm or washed up by it. I know Wotsit doesn't like the fireworks popping and fizzing above the sea, so I kept him in. Something has shifted in Violet though. She seems bigger, unruly. Though it's hard to tell, I think I perceive more of her creeping legs, as though they have multiplied. More complex shapes appear on her face, and I often allow her to dab her proboscis over my damp paint box, idly trying to sketch her as she does so. As a result, she has a greater repertoire of colours, and I have some strange paintings. I used to paint only from life, the landscapes of the shifting shoreline or the nature reserve, or perhaps a still life when the weather is off. Then, for the longest time, I painted nothing at all. But now, as I watch Violet suck in the paint, I will fill a sketchbook with lines and shapes that are suggested by her but come mostly from my imagination. It is impossible to paint her accurately, so I just let my brush move over the paper and create what it will.

As I put on my coat to join the others in the burning of the year's wreckage, she oozed over to me and began to insinuate herself into the deep recess of my tin cloth pocket. She has not been close to me in this way before, her heat against my leg, her worming shape.

"You can't come," I said, wondering, as I did, what the problem was. Would anybody see her? She is so difficult to perceive; I must try hard even though I have learned over the past few weeks. Could anyone else, not looking for her, see her in the cold and dark with the red and gold lights of the fireworks overhead? It's unfair that Wotsit can come and go, slinking around the last of the flowers in the garden, rubbing his chin against rusting, salvaged anchors gifted by Solomon. Violet spends most of the time in the grate, or inside the driftwood, which still just about accommodates her. But she came from out there, from the beach, from further than that. I had to let her out for some air.

My heart batted at my ribs. What would happen if someone else saw her? Maybe I secretly wanted someone else to see her, to tell me what to do. I sense her needs changing and that I won't be adequate soon; my paperbacks and dishes of water and paints. Outside we went, she: hot as a baked potato in my pocket, trembling, sliding about, me: cold-faced in the salty breeze. The bonfire was ablaze, crackling and shedding orange filaments. A small crowd gathered. Solomon was just beyond the shore in his fishing boat, launching the fireworks. Up they fizzed in bursts of Bismuth Yellow, Viridian and Silver. Off they shrieked, their papery debris falling into the sea. The Headland's children were especially beautiful under the glow, their breath misting the air, their upturned faces luminous. I wondered briefly what it would be like to clutch a little gloved hand in my own. But that is not going to happen for me now.

Seb stood close to me, drinking something from a plastic cup.

"Want a tipple? Warm you up?" he asked me. I told him no, thanks. He looked better. He said things were settling down, people had been worried about the power station, but nothing had happened so the idea was receding from their minds, joining the background of their thoughts. The storm will too, in time. Those that really worry about power stations, well, they tend not to live next to them.

"People don't get it," he said, "because of Chernobyl. That couldn't happen here." But there was a catch of doubt in his voice. He swigged more of his drink. I shrugged because I know anything can happen – even that. But I saw his point: people want their kettles and toasters and TVs. They want to listen to music and play computer games, to read at night and see in the winter. Seb shifted closer to me and bent down suddenly, so he could talk in a low voice and still be heard over the crackle and shriek of the fireworks.

"But," he said, "Sol and I were out the night of the storm. We'd…we'd been drinking, you know." He stroked the back of his head. "We came home very late as the wind was picking up. And I thought…" He paused and sipped his drink, staring at the flames. I felt Violet squirming in my pocket, and a kind of expansion. It was the heat.

"I thought I saw something, Dolores, on the beach, glowing in the dark, a piece of wood I think, but somehow doing something weird…It was so windy, Sol made me go inside his cottage to wait out the storm. I was worried; was it something from the plant, some part come off? It was too risky in the storm to look, so we waited until morning."

My head thrummed. All at once, Violet oozed out of my pocket like an invisible spill of blood, her creeping legs spun her through the air and into the bonfire. There was a flash of iridescence everyone missed. Seb went on as I peered into the crackling flames, my knees trembling.

"When morning came, we walked along the shore to find it, but then we saw grandma Irene's house and then we… we never went back. I've looked since, but nothing. But I wonder…"

The flames crackled indigo for a moment and leapt and everyone whooped. Seb muttered something about how there must have been some paint on the wood in there.

"You know, it was very confusing, the storm," I said. "There was lightning, and you were a little tipsy. I'm sure it was nothing."

He leaned in again, tall with that straight dark hair, black eyes pinpointed with orange from the fire. "The thing is, there are only certain things that glow like that. I'm not a top-level engineer. If something small, isolated, happened, I wouldn't be told. Or worse still, if something happened and nobody realised."

I swallowed and said in a low voice, "Why worry needlessly?"

"Because," he said, "something like that would be dangerous. It could contaminate people. And the Headland's community…the future of the power station…it…"

I've always liked the fact that the power station is here, with its marching forest of pylons disappearing over the horizon, and the warm waters creating a unique habitat for unusual fish. How it acts as a cliff face for birds on an otherwise flat peninsula. It both is and is not part of the landscape. But now I watch its glow from Watchbell's window and worry. If Violet comes from there, if she is somehow part of its miraculous science, none of us are safe. I looked into the bonfire, still colourless with fear for her. I knew she needed and liked heat, but what could I do now? How could I get her back?

"Are you alright, Dolores? You look a bit…? I didn't mean to scare you."

"Fine, fine," I muttered.

In the end, I waited. Waited deep into the night as the crowd dispersed and people went home to their mugs of tea and Thursday night Findus Crispy Pancakes. I thought about you whilst I crouched in the dark. What would you have made of it all? I waited until the bonfire had died down to twisted wood and ash. Then the sun started to come up. Sleep is for the weak. Violet was there, in the natural cage of the bonfire. I closed one eye to see her pulsing like a huge, transparent cumulonimbus, flashing her colours, the stain on her face copying an image of the grey waves touched by the yellow dawn.

"Come back," I said, and turned towards Watchbell, square and black in the distance, its garden now shedding its leaves and dropping its blooms. She followed me.

Saturday 21st November 1987, 5 a.m.

I can't sleep, so I have just decided to get up. Violet is doing what I think of as sleeping, shushing away in her driftwood. Only now, she is getting too big for it. The wood is developing fissures and cracks, and her light glows out of it all night. I should really sleep upstairs in my bedroom, where I have not slept since the storm, but I want to be near her. There is a scorch mark on the table. She stays in the fire most of the day, glowing and getting larger. Sometimes she goes to the back of the front door and tries to insinuate herself through the letterbox and outside. The viper's bugloss, so vibrantly purple when in flower in the summer, is skeletal, sticking up along the beach. The air is cold, and the nights draw in. Although she wants to be warm, I sense Violet needs to go out. But I am afraid of what will happen if somebody sees her. I keep thinking about what Seb said. He told me that anything radioactive needs to be buried. Chernobyl is covered by a huge carapace, a kind of sarcophagus.

I'm not sure Violet will be understood. She is benign, as far as I can tell. I am not afraid of her. I love talking to her and feeding her books and newspapers. I have somebody to care for now, someone who needs me. I like to watch the shapes and letters and numbers move across her face; though if she is trying to communicate, I still cannot understand her. I like being the one to keep her warm. But I know that she is growing, and that she desires more than I am giving her now. I am afraid *for* her, but on the other hand, she is almost impossible to see, especially if you are not looking for her. Nobody saw her at the bonfire, not even Seb, who was talking about her as she glowed inside it. Outside, oozing bedside me, the background of the rushing clouds and crackled seakale, the curling waves and the dusty wind would confuse the eye enough that even if you thought you saw something…

I went to the library yesterday after work, looking for a better encyclopaedia than the old one I have here, to try to work out if there are any creatures like her anywhere. When I looked, I saw that Violet has the characteristics of a Humboldt squid, with its ability to change colour, flashing brightly in the sea depending on its moods. But then, she also has the proboscis of a moth, who uses it to taste the air. But she doesn't have wings. The golden mole has iridescent fur, but it is not invisible. There are creatures that like very hot conditions, like camels, or weird bacteria called water bears, which live off thermal vents. These can also revert to a state of agelessness and defy the passage of time. Then, I looked at plant life. The violet flower: so many different species, some thriving where there is barely any soil. Her creeping legs which shift in and away from my perception as they move belong to nothing that I can identify. Only deep-sea creatures seem to possess this quality of transparency, the filaments of their nervous systems visible beneath their jelly-like skin. But these would be like deflated balloons outside of the water, and Violet has thrived on land for weeks now. I looked at insects, mammals, birds, cephalopods. Octopuses and squids have limbs that can perceive independently. Bees are especially attuned to the ultraviolet end of the spectrum, which humans cannot see, and so attracted by white and purple flowers. They communicate by vibration and strong smell, and movement. The bookworm, which is really a beetle, eats mould, glue and the bindings of books, only incidentally devouring the paper. Moths do that too. Some butterflies like decaying matter and live near graves...

I made a list of notes like a student cramming for a weird exam. Then, I looked at another section of the library. Next to the Science Fiction were titles like *Top Secret* and *The Many Types of Luminous Sky Phenomena*, *Alien Life*, and *We are not Alone: Alien Abduction Cases*. Some had facsimile documents from places like the FBI with chunks redacted in black ink, alien autopsy photos and pilot accounts of disc- or orb-like vessels. Sketches from abduction "victims" of thin grey men with big black screen eyes. If Violet is not of this world, she is not this kind of alien.

I have wondered if I am being haunted, though I don't believe in ghosts. And one doesn't bring a ghost into the house from outside, dragging it along the beach and hauling it over the threshold. A ghost dwells inside, and is already there.

Of course, I have to consider my own state of mind. I'm the only one who can see her, or at least has seen her. Some might say I have been through a lot lately. I'm not unaware of that. Of how it would seem to an outsider. Which is why, maybe, I haven't told anyone yet. But Seb talked of something glowing on the beach the night of the storm, and something in his voice, some catch of strange desire mixed in with his fear, makes me sure he encountered Violet.

The next thing I must do requires my courage. I must let her outside. I must work out, somehow, what she needs.

Don't forget: Lemon cake – 2 slices.

Milk and cat food.

Sunday 22nd November 1987. Night.

I went to see my mother again today. Took the bus along the coast. Some of the damaged roofs were repaired and the fallen trees have been taken away. I remembered the cake this time – hopped off the bus two stops early to go into the bakery on the high street. Mum has always liked the taste of lemons.

She didn't know me today, but she did really like me, greeting me as if I were a new member of staff, or someone else's relative. We sat for a while after our tea and cake, me listening to the click-clack of her knitting needles. Violet makes this soft clicking sound sometimes. I haven't figured out what it means.

"What would you do," I asked, "if you were looking after something and you knew it was important but not really what it actually was?"

Mum was always wise and measured before her illness, and often still is now.

"Like a piece of jewellery or some sort of computer gizmo thing?" she said.

"No, not an object; a living thing."

"Someone's baby? Did you find a baby?" She looked alarmed and put down her knitting.

"No, no. Like an animal, a creature, only it's not a creature you've ever seen before, and you don't know where it's from. Or where it belongs."

For a moment, I thought she didn't understand, so I stopped talking and just listened to the clicking needles, soft as a cricket at the window. Then she said, "You need an expert, someone who knows about animals. A vet or a biologist or whatever you call them."

I know this is the only sensible thing to do. But I said, "But what if you knew that the creature was not – not of this world? From somewhere entirely different? And that you might put them in danger if you told the wrong expert?"

Mum narrowed her eyes. "How would you know?"

"Because you feel it. You know it here." I tapped my chest. She sat back, eyeing me, and dropped a stitch.

"Ah, well: that's something else. In that case, if you're going to follow that course, you must follow it all the way."

She didn't say anything else, just continued to knit what looked to me like a hat, and one too small for any adult.

Tuesday 1st December 1987, 11 p.m.

This evening, at dusk, after my teaching, I arrived at Watchbell.

The plants are dying back now, the seakale small and dark, the viper's bugloss dry and the elder friable. There are old Michaelmas daisies, some faded, dry hydrangeas delicately mauve, crisping in the cold air. As I approached, I felt something was wrong: a vibration through my feet and a sound coming from the house. From the path, this sound was high pitched like a whistling kettle, and became shriller as I got closer. When I looked at the shingle, the top layer of stones was vibrating about an inch above the ground. I looked around. There was no-one in the blue-dark and the floating stones extended only around my cottage. I approached the yellow door with a shadowy feeling in my chest. The high-pitched sound was an unbearable shriek this close to the door and I could barely breathe. The blood thrummed in my head. Something terrible must be happening inside. I turned the key and pushed but some great weight behind the door resisted me. I put my shoulder into it and shoved with all my might, the adrenalin in my body giving me a strength I don't usually have. I pushed hard, three times, and felt on the third an unloosening. "Violet," I shouted. "Violet!" Something peeled away and came unstuck and I crashed through the doorway.

Violet was there, but I had to search for her; the sound was so loud, so piercing I could barely think. I closed one eye and scanned the room. I saw that in the kitchen all the glasses were broken, and I worried about Watchbell's windows, but they were intact. Then I saw her, flattened over the ceiling like a manta ray or a huge iridescent pancake. The sound continued. It got into my soul somehow and made me despair. The sides of my head were sharp with pain. Violet pulsed red; waves of colour passing over her flattened body. The fire was burning high in the grate as if she'd added fuel to it somehow. There were pieces of paper all over the floor, like confetti at the strangest of weddings.

"Stop," I whispered, "please stop. I'll take you outside. I'll take you right now."

Who knows if she understands me, but she stopped and a wave of green passed over her. Then she shrank down to her more compact size and looped her way down from the ceiling. I didn't take off my coat. I took her outside right then, trembling with fear and relief. We went out into the dark. She followed me along the beach rolling her many legs across the stones, flashing in and out of my perception. She copied the shapes of the dark clouds across her face. She click-clacked like my mother's needles. We walked for an hour. The only lights when we returned were in the windows of the cottages, the glow of the power station, and the scoping beam of the lighthouse. We returned and Violet oozed back into her driftwood and shushed loudly for the rest of the evening.

For the first time in weeks, I decided to sleep in my bed upstairs, and it was when I pulled back the covers that I saw Wotsit, ears drawn back, eyes wide, still reeling from the violent happenings earlier. Sad puss, I thought, and stroked him until he slept.

Wednesday 16th December 1987. Lunchtime.

A break in my timetable at work, and I find myself missing Violet. Watchbell House is a bit of a mess inside: punched out paper everywhere, ashes and soot from the constant fire in the grate. I think that Violet is getting too cold. Whilst she loves to come out with me now, when we return, she goes straight to the fire and she likes the flames high. Her body quivers and phases, and somehow, she adds more oxygen, so it quickly gets hot. I'm in the cottage in a T-shirt in December, but Wotsit seems to like it and curls up close by, watching the flames. I have become fairly confident in taking Violet for walks; the days are short and the weather often cold and drizzly, so we don't meet many others walking. Those that we do often have dogs, and the dogs (who seem to be able to see or smell Violet) will raise their hackles or growl or cower, looking at the blank space beside me. Their owners, who can't see anything, are apologetic, laughing nervously: "He's never usually like this…" And so, we are not disturbed. There is a thrill, a feeling inside me that I have a secret, and the dangerous idea (I know it is dangerous) that Violet is mine and mine alone, and that I must therefore be special.

We usually walk the beach, taking in the two lighthouses: one black, austere and defunct, just a tower for tourists, and the other still working: small, white and blue and sitting at the edge of the shingle beach. As the sky darkens, we see its light sliding across the sea. We go past the wrecked boats, like animal skeletons; and the working boats; the dirty yellow machinery that levels the shingle; and the Headland's odd little houses and chalets, every one a different style, inhabited by locals, artists, writers and visitors. Rusted anchors, sheep skulls and World War II shrapnel decorate the various shingle gardens.

On a recent walk, a surprisingly bright Sunday with a suggestion of frost in the air, we went to the nature reserve, stopping off at the various hides along the route. Violet stayed close, sometimes flickering in the air, sometimes tracking along the ground on her shifting legs, sometimes oozing around the stones and logs. The hides look out onto the lake and the concrete slab of the power station. There are grebes and swans, but we also saw a bittern and heard its distinctive *boom* from the fenland. In the hedges, bright finches, electric-blue damsel flies, their bright engines humming, soft-bodied peacock butterflies with their false gazes and silky wings. But I thought afterwards, this isn't the time of year for these creatures.

On a final loop, we went to see the sound mirrors. I often take my students to paint them. Concrete structures, built in the mid-twenties, separated from the public by a corridor of lake water and the locked swing bridge that is opened a few days a year for photographers. They were created to catch the sound of enemy aircraft. The three you can see are a huge, curved wall; a concave dome, thirty feet high, like a huge dark ear tuned to the sky; and a smaller cave-like arc. They became defunct when radar was introduced but are, even graffitied, eerily beautiful, crowned with birds that use them like cliffs. They still work, and if you had the skill and the right kind of stethoscope you could sit at their feet with them curving above you and hear planes miles away concealed in the clouds, or boats rolling towards the shore. Or pigeons and sparrows, grebes and the occasional kestrel.

Whilst I stood there, gazing out at these ghostly monuments as if they were a set of portals to the past, Violet climbed up my torso, via the toggles on my coat – something she has never done before. I felt her hot, vibrating form through the cloth, and as the vibrating continued, soft but steady, I swear it was picked up by those huge concrete structures and all the birds rose, cawing and confused, away and into the sky. The pitch of the sound began to drop, then the volume increased. It came from her but had been taken up by the mirrors. I put my hands over my ears. I couldn't stand it. Lower and lower. I felt it in my blood, my organs, so low, and then I couldn't hear it at all but felt it through the ground. Then it stopped and Violet oozed away from me. I stumbled back along the path and noticed two things: ripples on the lake, circles of disturbance though there was no wind, and several butter-flies, painted lady, peacock and cabbage white, flapping impotently on the path as if they had forgotten how to fly. Butterflies that had survived the start of winter.

Once home, I noticed a hardness to Violet's usually amor-phous outline as she warmed herself in the fire. Across her face flashed the outlines of the sound mirrors, as if she could not stop thinking about them.

Tuesday 22nd December 1987. Winter Solstice. Late.

A strange time of year, the darkest day over and the days about to slowly lengthen. I always think this is the coldest time, but that is still to come in January and February, pos-sibly into March, when the plants in the shingle begin to revive. Violet spent a lot of time in the fire today, only com-ing out to vaporise the dishes of water I set out for her. The sea was choppy last night, but is still and has receded today, the sky dark with low cloud that refuses to give up its rain. I put dinner to slow cook in the oven after school and then I went for a walk alone to catch the last of the light. Violet doesn't want to move from the fire anyway. Images from our past walks cycle across her face and her limbs flash in the flames. She is imprinted with the shapes of the clouds, words from the labels on my food jars, the silhouettes of gulls and cormorants.

I needed some time to myself, just a stroll along the shingle past the artists' studios and workers' cottages, the rusted ornaments of world wars, propellers and spent shells now sculptural, threaded with the tendrils of dying plants, emerging now to be covered again when vegetation takes over in the spring. As I crunched along, I felt tired. I have been sleeping only lightly, filled with weird dreams and half listening for Violet to scream again as she once did. But since I have walked her regularly like some amorphous dog, she has settled. It was only the sound mirrors that elicited those vibrations.

I saw Solomon in the distance tidying away his nets, pulling them up towards the white clapboard cottage he lives in. No sign of his brother Seb, who often goes over to see Sol for a drink, but it was early and a weekday. They might be saving themselves for Christmas. Strings of coloured lights behind me in Gold Stone, a livelier seaside town (though not by much). Christmas. The beach was churned by last night's unsettled waves, and the cold blasted my cheeks. Then I saw, half covered in shingle, something hard and round, like a huge black egg doming from the stones. I tapped it with my foot to loosen the shingle and realised quickly that it was a bomb, old, rusted and coated in barnacles. I instinctively ran up the beach to Solomon's place. The Headland is filled with old washed-up legacy from the war; much of it decorates the shingle gardens. I have heard of bombs needing to be detonated at sea in controlled explosions, but until today I had never seen one as large as this.

I reached Solomon's door out of breath and knocked hard, casting my eye back to the bomb that I could barely make out in the dark over the expanse of shingle. He took his time, opening the door slowly, a mug of something steaming in his grip. His perpetual frown softened when he saw me.

"Dolly," he said gently. "Come in."

"No…" I began. "It's…" And I pointed down the beach and started to explain. He looked over my shoulder and pulled me into the house.

"Come in. It might be very dangerous. Is there anyone else out walking?"

"Not that I saw. It's not really the night for it." A fire burned in the grate in Solomon's front room. I was glad Violet wasn't with me, snaking around in my pocket, longing for warmth. Solomon called the coastguard and sat me down with a whisky whilst we waited for the bomb disposal team. They told us not to approach it. I sat across from Solomon on a hard, Formica chair at a beaten metal table with salvaged wooden legs. There was a tang of brine in the air that always clings about Sol, but it was not unpleasant, mixing with the harsh malt of the whisky in my nostrils. I felt warm and slightly lightheaded.

"How are you?" I asked him, thinking of his grandmother's recent funeral, Irene scattered on the wind.

"Alright, Dolores. Doing okay. You know I prefer spring and summer; it's better when I can fish all day and into the evening. Now I find myself idle. I've seen Claire a bit. She speaks highly of your art classes."

This last seemed difficult for him to say. His daughter has his same wild dark curls, but long and falling down her back, or piled on her head with a pencil pushed through them. She's already showing talent as an artist, but she's into thick pastels and oil paints, she hasn't much time for the vulnerability of water colours. Her fingers are always stained. I've noticed she has no truck with the banter of her peers and wants to get on with things. She curls her lip when they talk over my instructions. I told him she's a great artist already and a red flush crept over his neck.

"Why don't you come over?" I found myself saying. "After the bomb is sorted. I've got a pie in the oven and it's too much for one."

"Okay," he said, and supped his whisky. "If they don't take all night."

In the end they came to the door an hour or so later, torches moving up the beach in the dark, blotched stars above them. They were both wearing rigid vests and carrying helmets under their arms. One was shorter than the other, but both had wide, impassive faces.

"Come and have a look," one said. "False alarm really, so you can." He offered this like it was a fairground attraction. We went out, wrapped against the cold. Solomon lent me a coarse woollen hat; I had forgotten mine and the temperature had dropped.

"It's an old sea mine. Second World War." They had dug it out of the shingle, and it was dark grey and greenly barnacled, the shape of an old-fashioned diver's helmet but four times bigger.

"Very dangerous if it still had its fuses, but it doesn't; they're probably on the seabed." One of the men leant against it and lit a cigarette, its tip glowing hot in the dark night. As it is so heavy, they left it, saying that the council might want it for the maritime museum in Gold Stone, but otherwise it might just be another Headland curiosity, another piece of sculptural salvage for the tourists to take moody photos of. I was disappointed. I longed for the controlled explosion at sea lighting the water up white-hot, making huge waves to churn the shore.

"Thanks for calling us out though. With its fuses it would have been pretty lethal," said the shorter one.

The tall one added, "If one exploded, you'd kiss goodbye to every cottage here. And the power station; well, it doesn't bear thinking about. So, you did the right thing."

I regretted my invitation to Solomon as we trekked back to Watchbell House. It wasn't that messy today, but what if Violet didn't remain sedately warming herself in the fire?

But only I can see her so nothing could happen. Sol stood with his hands in his pockets, looking down, as I opened the door.

"It's a bit of a state," I said.

"Don't worry about it; it's nice to be invited." His eyes went straight to the floor of the main room, which was littered with bits of paper.

"It's for an art project," I said. "It's sort of experimental."

But the kitchen was clean, the pie was in the oven and Violet pulsed quietly in the grate.

"You left your fire burning?"

"I just don't like it cold when I come in. I thought I was only out for a short walk…"

Sol shrugged and sat on the sofa, scooping Wotsit up like he was made of cloth, and rubbing his hands over his fur.

"Smells good in here, like lemons. Are you burning something scented in that fire?"

"No," I said, staring down at the pie whilst I dished it up. He couldn't see her, but he could smell her as I could. I took a deep breath. "Might just be the wood."

Sol kept looking at the floor and towards the window, perhaps to where the fissured driftwood sat on the table. We ate together, silently at times, but we also talked about the Headland recovering after the storm, about painting and his daughter Claire, about fishing stocks and repairing his boat. Randy is having a New Year's Eve party at Café Ferdinand and Solomon said I should go.

"And Christmas day; do you have plans?"

"I'll see my mum," I said, which was true. "And then I'm with friends in town," which was a lie. I don't like to lie but I know people around here whisper about me: lonely Dolores without a family. Tragic Dolores with no one to spend Christmas with. I don't care that much, but I don't want Sol to think of me that way.

He was in the city, he said, with cousins. I could tell he didn't really want to go, would hate the smog and the traffic and miss the salty air and open sky.

"Seb's coming. He likes the city, likes to get away sometimes. He's been edgy since the storm."

"How so?" I asked, blowing a piece of hot meat and pastry.

"Just worried about the reactor. The Chernobyl thing doesn't help. And letters they've been getting. Protestors. You're always going to get that though. But it's like he half believes them, has lost his trust." I'd given Sol wine in a mug, since Violet's scream had shattered the glassware. He gulped it like tea. "It's so hot in here, Dolly; how much is on that fire?" I noticed then the sweat on his brow and upper lip, shining in the orange light. He pulled off his heavy jumper.

I told him I'd let it burn down, but of course Violet was keeping the flames up. He squinted over at it, then suddenly got up and bent down to the flames.

"It's okay," I said, jumping to my feet. "Just leave it for now. Don't forget your pie…"

"Looks like you might have a crack there, in the fire clay, just there." He closed one eye and pointed directly at Violet. Just one line of her mutable outline had hardened as I'd noticed the other day, whilst the rest of her remained intangible. But I panicked for a moment that Solomon was peering so intently that he'd learn the trick of seeing her. If anyone else could, I felt it would be him. I knew he was starting to tune into her existence. Solomon saw the hardening line as a fissure at the back of the fire. He didn't twig. Why would he? But Violet is becoming unstable. Or stable I suppose, to look at it another way; hardening into reality. I told Sol I was tired and maybe if he didn't mind…It had been a strange evening; it was pretty late now.

"Okay, I'm sorry," he said, his hand on the latch, dark brows knotted again.

"I'll come," I said as he walked down the path. He frowned again.

"To the New Year's Eve party. I'll see you there."

The day of Dolores's funeral. Morgan fiddles with his tie in the bedroom mirror; the knot looks wonky whatever he does. He starts sweating and gives up. A text from Maggie: *Thinking of you today x.*

The funeral takes place at the little white church above the dunes. Morgan is overwhelmed by the purple and white flowers all over the pews: viper's bugloss identical to the ones thriving on the beach, irises and scented white roses, airy sprigs of baby's breath. The wicker coffin is closed. The church is almost full. Morgan nods to Randy in her elegant black suit, and Claire, curls tied back, embraces him at the door. "This is my dad, Solomon," she says. A man with a shock of curly white hair steps forwards and shakes his hand. His forearms are knotty with muscle and his body is wiry and robust, though he must be in his eighties. His eyes are bright and black, his cheeks red with broken capillaries – wind scorched.

"Hello, Morgan, you probably don't remember me. I moved away from the Headland, but sometimes I visited, and your mother let me take you out on the fishing boat."

Solomon is familiar; Morgan remembers a boat trip, the glittering blue horizon and the slap of fish into the hull, pulling up crab nets and tight fishing lines, the counter-power of the water. Fish entrails slopping onto the boat as Solomon sliced them open with a silver blade. The rich, briny smell of the sea and the stench of fish blood.

"It's good to see you, Solomon." Morgan thinks of the diary; he knows the younger Solomon from there. He feels strange, having this secret. The music plays, Beethoven's *Für Elise*, and they take their seats. No vicar for his mother, but a humanist celebrant who talks about her returning to the landscape, how her ashes will be scattered at sea, how her life is to merge with nature. Morgan's ears are buzzing as if full of insects. He agreed to give a speech, but now he doesn't want to. Only his younger self, with whom he has lost touch, knows these people. They are unfamiliar as por-traits in a gallery. His shirt is sticking to his back. He stands in front of his mother's body and addresses them.

"I…err…thank you for coming along today to remember my mother, Dolores Poole. I know she loved it here on the Headland, so much so I think she considered it her real home. But also, in a way, this was a secret for her, a re-treat away from town. Somewhere to spend her summers, to paint in and enjoy the garden." Morgan pauses, takes a breath. There are tears coming, but they are not related to the speech, rather an image of their last meeting and the rush of time and how it seems to be leaving him behind, when all of the people in front of him, looking at him, are somehow enmeshed in it, held, part of it.

"It's good to know how loyal her friends have been, how much she could rely on you all. She was inspired to paint here too. I'll admit, this is an unusual landscape: the stony beach, the heat, the power station…" There is faint laughter from the church, an exchange of wry smiles. "But the landscape appealed to her heart...I hope to see you at dusk, when we send her into the landscape she loved."

Morgan looks around the church before sitting down, trying to find a face that reminds him of his own.

Christmas Day 1987. Midnight.

I saw Mum today. She had knitted me a hat in dark purple shot through with yellow patterns. Christmas dinner was served at *The Lilacs* at twelve p.m., with a lit-up pudding and a glass of sherry afterwards. The dining room was full of people eating slowly and the smell of sprouts and gravy. I noticed some people didn't have family visiting them, so the staff had grouped them together and sat with them, adjusting the paper crowns they had got from their crackers and talking softly.

"Where's Adrian, Dolly? He comes to us every Christmas. And your sister. Are they late? Do you think I cooked the turkey for too long? It seems dry."

Mum munched her dinner, thinking she was at home a few Christmases ago when we all used to congregate in the cramped front room. She didn't seem concerned though.

"You and I can have a nice drink in peace," she said, and squeezed my hand. I painted her a watercolour of Watchbell House and framed it as a gift, squat black with its jaunty primrose yellow windows, frayed clouds in the sky and snow over the shingle. This last I imagined as it rarely snows, except a smattering in February sometimes, but I wanted it to be festive.

"Where is this?" she asked.

"You know, the weekend house, the summer house. Except that I'm living there now."

"I bet Adrian hates it, why aren't you at your house?" She sat up in her chair. "Is it a money thing? If it is then…"

"No, no. The thing is…" She'd forgotten about the breakup and I didn't want to upset her on Christmas Day, so I said, "He…we're just in it for Christmas. We thought it would be cosy with the fire and everything."

The lie sat heavy with me. Sometimes I omitted the truth, but I rarely lied to Mum. Tomorrow she could remember every detail of what happened between me and Adrian, and she could remember the lie as well. Her life is confusing enough. I drank my weak coffee in silence with an After Eight mint. Then she started up on a memory and chatted away: me and Cassie so excited one Christmas Day we woke up at four a.m. and were found at six surrounded by torn coloured paper, under the tree. We were so tired by mid-morning we fell asleep and missed lunch. Or the time, grown up, Cassie came to stay from Seattle and her baby, Joel, cried all night and the adults were all asleep by lunch, slumped over one another on the sofas whilst the Queen's speech played, ignored, on the television. I remembered games of charades, tubes of sweets and terrible Christmas comedy specials. The feeling that nobody would leave, and these Christmas Days would never change. She hugged me when I left *The Lilacs*. Her small back felt hard and frail and her paper crown crinkled against my ear. I hated to leave her, but it was dark already and the staff were getting ready for the evening routine, for Christmas TV: *The Two Ronnies* and an Agatha Christie film had won the residents' vote. "I love a mystery," Mum said as she waved me goodbye.

I expected my evening to be quiet; I'd have a drink and watch *Ghostbusters*, all ectoplasm and sarcasm, and worry about Violet, whose outline was becoming visible. But when I approached Watchbell House, I saw Adrian's car parked on the shingle and a light on inside. He still had his key; Watchbell is technically half his. He was on the sofa with a coffee and Wotsit, staring at the fire. I realised Violet wasn't in the fire. Or spread across the ceiling above him. Or glowing in her fissured driftwood. My voice stuck in my throat.

"Merry Christmas, Dol." He held up his mug.

"Hi." I asked him why he was here and gave him a brief hug. He smelt of whisky, but it is Christmas.

"I just wanted to see you. I've been here a while, so I just started a fire. It's really chilly eh?"

"You didn't have plans for Christmas Day?"

"No. Well I have plans for tomorrow, but I thought you might be on your own today."

My breath shuddered around in my throat. Christmas wasn't meant to be like this for us, and I felt it physically: the burning sensation of loss in my limbs. Was it a pity visit? But I wondered if he might be lonely himself. Was he thinking about what might have been, of a life we almost had but didn't? Maybe the new girlfriend and the glamorous city life I had imagined for him are not what they are cracked up to be. He told me the job was okay, he had been lucky, but the stock market crash had made things tricky. His colleagues had lost their confidence, and many had lost their jobs.

"It used to be fun," he said, as I stuck some frozen burgers under the grill and hunted in the cupboard for a tin of beans: a child's meal. "Too much fun, I think at times: long boozy lunches with clients and loud banter and swaggering on the trading floor. We're all a bit humbled."

I was panicking. I made an excuse to go upstairs, but no Violet. My chest hurt and my forearms tingled. I shifted the driftwood on the table in the pretence of making room for supper, but it felt hollow, cold and dry. I took deep breaths. I didn't want Adrian to leave like last time. I missed his lopsided mouth and sleepy eyes, holiday stubble, and his jumper with the sleeves rolled up. If she was gone, she was gone. I could only hope she had escaped on a walk because I had been away all day and that she would come back when she was cold. I could only hope, in the dark, nobody would see that hardening outline. I resolved to be sociable with Adrian and to go out later to find her.

"Sorry, not exactly a Christmas meal," I said as I dished out the food. "I had one actually, with Mum, at the nursing home."

"How is she?" he said, settling into his chair and taking a bite of his burger.

"She's okay," I said after a pause. "Still Mum but she can't remember certain things, doesn't know what year she's in. It's like she lives inside memories and jumps between them. As if…as if time is different or even meaningless. I don't know," I sipped my mug of wine. "It's hard to explain."

"Where are the glasses?"

"Oh, I'm clumsy these days. I keep breaking them."

He looked at me, cheap burger juice dripping onto his plate, leaning down to his food as he always does, his torso too long to be comfortable at a table. I imagined Violet oozing over his shoulders.

"You know, maybe your mum has the right idea; it's not good to remember everything…Do you think she'd like a visit from me?"

I told him that she often thought he and I were still together; she had not made any new memories for the past couple of years. He would confuse her, or worse still, we might have to act out a lie.

"I'm still your friend, Dolores."

He reserves my full name for more serious moments. And for moments when he knows he's telling a half-truth. I suddenly realised he was visiting me to say goodbye, not out of pity but as a final farewell, that there probably was some other life he was leading now. I thought of the Christmas we might have had, if things had been different. If you were here. But he had left me completely. He wasn't going to say it out loud; the visit itself was the message and I saw it all in his face. My eyes filled up, but I just went to the kitchen for some more wine and breathed the tears away before I turned to face him again.

We watched *Indiana Jones and the Temple of Doom* on the sofa. We'd seen it in the cinema when it came out, arms looped together, laughing and crunching popcorn. Now, it seemed so different as I watched it again. Grotesque. I stared as the strange priest ripped someone's heart out with his bare hands and held it there, pulsating and bloody. When the credits rolled, Adrian got up and pulled me into a bear hug.

"See you soon," he said, and wrapped himself into his coat, fishing in his pocket for car keys. I knew then I'll never see him again. As he drove away, the engine a loud purr on the windy coast, I saw his set of Watchbell keys left on the table, between the driftwood and his half-finished mug of wine.

I rushed out of the house without my coat on with the best torch – the one for power cuts and other emergencies. I ran around the beach, breathless, shining the beam over everything: old seakale like cabbages and the shadows of dry viper's bugloss like skeletal fingers in the dark. Then I looked to the sea rattling back and forth on the shore and saw a spherical shape rising, glowing blue in the darkness. The sea mine. For a moment, I thought the bomb team were wrong, but then there was no logic that would make it glow, even if it was live. I ran closer. It was Violet, stretched around the mine like a shining skin, embracing it.

"Violet?" I breathed, and she coalesced with the sound of a bath emptying, back into the creeping being I have become used to. Another part of her outline had hardened. I looked around the beach but saw nobody. The cottages glowed with fires and lamps in the distance, everyone having a final drink at the end of Christmas Day. She looked diminished somehow; the shapes moving across her face were sluggish and vague. She followed me back to Watchbell House and I realised how cold I was without my coat and gloves, my hands especially burning with pain as we got back into the warm front room. I expected Violet to go straight to the fire, so I sat on the sofa rubbing my hands together.

But she came over to me, closer and closer until I saw on her face an image of my own face; just a shadowy sketch, but unmistakably me, with my one high dimple and long nose, my bottom lip slightly larger than the top, my almond eyes and wavy hair. She drew closer still and I drew back, but she kept coming until she was over me and I saw myself in her, through her, and then she wrapped herself around my cold body. I felt her strange texture on my skin, like warm water, and the low, hot thrum of her frequency everywhere in my body. It was a feeling of bliss and timelessness, as if I floated across her or inside her. The smell of lemons and smoke, like a fire burning everything into vapour.

Then I fell into a deep sleep and woke up about an hour later. Violet glowed in the fire, her hardening outlines fading again, a clear image, like an ink sketch, of the barnacled sea mine printed on her face. I went to get her water and Christmas cards to feed on.

New Year's Day 1988. Early.

I've got hot, sweet coffee, my second cup of the day. Violet glows steadily in her driftwood. It's very cold: frost flowers on the windows, a dusting of white on the salvage that decorates the garden, a spider web that looks crafted from wire. Wotsit is like a hot water bottle in my lap. I need to wash, to fill up a steaming bath and add some lavender and climb in. I will. The new year has started. What will it hold? It's so different from the year I have just passed through (or that has passed through me). Last year brought the storm. It brought Violet. It took Irene away on the wind and scattered her into the sea. It took Adrian away and back to the city for good and gave me his half of Watchbell House, our holiday home, now just mine to live in with Wotsit and Violet. It brought an old bomb and left it on the beach. It was so different from the year before, which brought with it its own strangeness and took so much away from me.

There is a faint taste on my lips and a feeling on my skin, and the smell of someone else on my unwashed hair.

Last night I went to Café Ferdinand for Randy's New Year's Eve party. It was movie themed. I went as Princess Leia, somewhat half-heartedly: a white rollneck jumper and my hair pulled into loops at the side of my head. Randy greeted me as Rita Hayworth and handed me some punch.

"You look beautiful," I said. She beamed at me.

"I was Rita in another life: I'm convinced of it… Everybody's here. I'm so glad to see you. Solomon – I think he's meant to be Al Pacino from *The Godfather* but you'd hardly know it. And Seb…"

"He's Egon from *Ghostbusters*."

Seb had on a beige boiler suit with a cardboard backpack that he'd drawn buttons onto, and various bits of tin foil tubing. He and Sol had got there early, it seemed to me, and had got a head start on the drinking. They were laughing. As I approached, I saw the deep wrinkles around Sol's eyes.

"It took me ages to make this," said Seb, pulling the silver tube from his backpack out of his brother's hands. They turned and raised their glasses to me.

As the night went on, the whole community drifted in and out, filling the café with a chatter which rose above the cheesy music: Tony, the vicar and his wife; several of the artists and writers who don't live on the Headland full time but retreat to the cottages and converted railway carriage over Christmas; Solomon's daughter, Claire, looking older in a sparkling green dress with her curls piled up. She was a little embarrassed to talk to me, but Sol put his arm around her, his heart full with her being there. He drove her home before midnight and I watched them leave, a blast of cold air whistling through the café door behind them.

"So," said Randy (Rita) leaning across the counter and offering me cheese and pineapple on a stick, "what are your New Year's resolutions?"

I was taken aback by the question. The only thing I have thought about is keeping Violet alive and hidden from the world. I have thought about her changing and how I might be failing her in some way. I have spent most of my time with her, when not teaching my art students, letting her absorb my paints with her proboscis, letting her lick the very words from every printed surface in the house. In turn I have made numerous attempts to paint her ever-shifting form in water colours and oils, only ever producing some uninterpretable collection of lines and colours. I have walked her around the shingle beach and nature reserve and fed the fire to keep her warm. Cared for her. I have thought so little about myself and somehow that has been good for me.

I felt a presence at my side, and Solomon, smelling of the cold night air, was leaning on the counter.

"She's going to paint more," he said, winking at me. He grinned, taking a sip from the glass proffered by Randy. "Come spring, she'll be back on the beach painting the clouds, painting my fishing boat."

"That's it," I agreed, glad for once that someone spoke for me.

"And you, Sol?" asked Randy, wiping the counter and pouring herself a steaming mulled wine. Solomon's bluster left him like a storm blown out.

"Ah, I don't know." He stared darkly into his drink. "One of those hot wines after this?"

"Hardly takes you far into next year. I have the same resolution every New Year's Eve: have fun, be kind. That's it and it'll do."

She whirled away to refresh people's drinks and left us there. Sol's eyes were sleepy, and I felt tired looking at him. I tried to make conversation. Sometimes he just seems to close, like a door, leaving you in a room with no light where before… He turned to face me, black eyes almost pupil-less, dark stubble and the smell of frost and brine on his skin.

"They're going to leave that sea mine there on the shore. Council don't want the hassle and expense of moving it and think the summer tourists will like it. Could make a good painting; it's beautiful in its way."

"Your daughter could paint it," I said, thinking he might like to talk about her. His eyes brightened.

"Oh, she would. I just dropped her at her mum's. She wanted to stay until midnight but, you know, she's only sixteen." He reached over the counter then and drew a ladle of mulled wine from the cauldron of it bubbling at the bar. He slopped it into his half-finished whisky and drank it hot as if it couldn't burn his mouth. "She looks a bit like me," he said, "but with all her talents from elsewhere, her mother I suppose. I'm lucky Claire wants to spend time with me."

I don't know Sol's ex, but I see a lot of him in Claire: the stormy eyes and the wild curls, but also deeper things, a quiet core hiding a passion, something kept at bay because of its power, a defiance of order. He kept talking, tongue loosened by the mix of drinks and my nodding, my lack of comment or judgment. He told me about how he'd met Claire's mother. He was in his twenties but still as immature as a teenager, and she even younger than him. A summer spent hiding behind sand dunes and in old fishing boats to be with each other, no thought to the consequences. "Like rabbits we were; all raging hormones and in love with each other's bodies." I laughed to hear Solomon talk like this, but I also imagined his sunburned trainee-fisherman's body, naked amongst the seaweed and nets in the back of a rusty boat; salty skin and snogging.

"Her father was going to kill me. That's why my nose is broken." He pushed the end of his nose to show me the cartilage springing down and back. "I deserved it."

They had tried to be together, even got engaged and moved into a flat in town that the council helped with. "I wasn't prepared at all for the baby, for Claire. But the wonder of it, her tiny hands. Even when she cried and wouldn't sleep, my heart felt huge; I was breathless with love for her. The fucking gorgeous shape of her head with a fluff of dark hair on it. The smell of her. Her feet before they'd ever been walked on…Even her shits…"

He looked at me then, and his eyes woke up for a moment. "I don't mean to bring things up for you, Dolly," he muttered.

"Go on," I said, "I like to hear about it."

"No…Well, her mum and me, we realised we didn't love each other." He took a big gulp of his drink. "We were kids.

But we loved her. So, it's okay and we're friends. I suppose I'm just…I would love just to see Claire every day. I'm even jealous of you teaching her, seeing a side of her that I don't, helping her make beautiful things. How daft is that?"

"It's not," I said. I understand that biting jealousy when you want someone all to yourself. I thought of Violet; her heart-shaped face flashed into my mind. I told Sol I needed to go home.

We both realised that whilst we'd been talking midnight had come and gone, there was a rowdy countdown we'd dimly heard, and now everyone was cheering. He insisted on walking me home. I let him. I knew Violet was weak and cold, languishing in the fire, and I would say goodbye to him at the door. The Headland's wind was like a blade, slicing right into my chest and fingertips despite layers of my mother's wool. The shingle crackled beneath our feet and I held Sol's arm, to steady him rather than me.

But I didn't leave him at the yellow door to Watchbell House. As I turned to go in, he put his arm against the frame and leaned over me, his eyes warm and lit by the glow of my living room. I grabbed the collar of his coat and pulled his big, shadowed face down to me and kissed him, inhaling the scent of cloves and cinnamon on his breath, and something else like sea salt. His face was flushed in the chill air and I felt the thump of his big, steady heart as I drew him through the door. Violet flashed electric blue for a moment in the grate and I looked at her and smiled as I led Solomon upstairs.

He was gone before dawn, out trawling the cold, dark sea, no doubt.

Morgan is immersed in the diary now, addicted to finding out what happens next. He has been reading it all afternoon in the cool living room of Watchbell House, avoiding the heat and putting off as long as possible going to Café Ferdinand for his mother's wake. She'll be ready soon, burnt to ash, and he'll have to go and collect her for the evening's procession along the beach. Then he'll have to talk to people over warm beer and finger foods. At least there are no relatives to see; his aunt Cassandra is too frail to come over from the States. She wouldn't want to anyway, never one for acknowledging emotions. Never one for grief. He need only mingle with the Headlanders, who were dear friends to his mother and whom she seemed to love the most. He is both keen and afraid to talk to Solomon.

Later, having collected it from the baby-faced humanist, Morgan is carrying the urn along the sea path, back towards the beach and Café Ferdinand. The urn is dark blue with a swirling pattern of green, polished and very light. He pictures his mother's dead body burning, her fine skin and brown hair (so short, having grown back only as down after the chemo), her pale green dress, curling in the fire, heating down to just this pot of dark, flaky ash. At one of his last meetings with her, she was propped up in bed at the hospice, her lips cracked and dry, her skin grey. But it was the smell of the room that got Morgan: sweet and acrid, a scent he wanted to turn away from, the smell of her body already dying before she herself had fully left him. She still smiled. She still managed a few gentle, funny words, though she kept pushing the button on her morphine drip long after the dose allowed had run out. Click, click, her finger went, until she drifted off to sleep. Three days later, he was with her as she died, her breaths huffing and sighing, getting further and further apart, her fingers wrapped around his own.

Café Ferdinand is filled with chatter and the clinking of glasses. He walks in, the urn held with both hands against his chest, and the room falls quiet for a moment. People raise their glasses in his direction and smile. Randy approaches him, hands him a beer and a plate of food, whilst taking the urn from him and placing it on the counter.

"That will start to get heavy," she says, placing a hand on his back. Around the walls of the American-themed café hang, somewhat incongruously, several abstract watercolour paintings with bizarre shapes and amorphous blendings of colour. Claire comes over with her father, who raises a beer to Morgan, nods and takes a long pull. Claire squeezes Morgan's shoulder.

"How kind of you to share some of your paintings for the wake," Morgan says. "Different from the ones in your gallery…"

Claire frowns for a moment, then laughs lightly. "Oh no; they're not mine. These are your mum's."

"She gave me these," says Randy. "In particular to display tonight. Said they were the most important paintings she'd made, but that she'd never shown them to anyone. Said it seemed fitting for today. I'm not sure why she kept them hidden – I think I like them most of all her work."

"We were all a bit surprised, to be honest," joins Claire.

Morgan sits down on a bar stool, unable to speak for a moment. Randy and Claire look at one another, then move away, busying with glasses and passing around plates of food. Morgan takes in the paintings. These must be sketches of Violet, the ones referred to in the diary. Although they might appear abstract, there is the suggestion of a heart or clover shape that repeats in many of them, a fan of moving limbs, flashes of light and a dominance of purple that chimes with Dolores's descriptions.

Solomon settles on a stool next to Morgan, crunching a portion of whitebait. Their little black eyes stare up from the plate.

"I'm sure you're with your own thoughts this evening, Morgan," he says, his pale curls stark above his deep black eyes and dark eyebrows, "But I wanted to ask you, later on, when the time comes, would you like to be on the boat with me? We can take her out –" he pats the urn – "out to sea where the ashes will be taken on the wind."

Morgan examines Solomon's face, the deep wrinkles and scorched cheeks, the clear dark eyes and long, elegant nose with its slightly broken line.

"I'd like to come, if that's okay."

Solomon breaks into a sad smile.

"She's your mother, Morgan, it is very much okay." He pauses, crunches another whitebait; it goes in head first. "We'll wait for darkness, then the procession will start."

Darkness comes late in summer, and when it does, it is tinged with indigo, and only a few of the very brightest stars can be seen. Dolores's friends are walking along the beach with paper lanterns singing "The Parting Glass" as the shingle crunches beneath their feet. Solomon pushes out the fishing boat, climbs in and secures a heavy life jacket across Morgan's shoulders.

…But since it falls unto my lot

That I should rise and you should not

I'll gently rise and I'll softly call

Good night and joy be with you all…

The voices, some beautiful and some tuneless, fade as the fishing boat moves out, water sloshing against its hull. It smells of crabs and salt, of fresh blood and the depths of the sea.

"It's a long time since I took her out," says Solomon quietly. Morgan holds the urn against his chest. When should he take off the lid? He sees the paper lanterns out on the edge of the beach, the lights of the cottages and the power station beyond, the dark waves between them. The puttering motor of the boat stops. It is time. He is surprised the ashes inside the urn are also inside a polythene bag. He puts his hand in.

"I wanted to say, I cared for your mother deeply," says Solomon. His voice is gruff, as if clogged with saltwater, his eyes clearer in the sea-darkness than Morgan has ever seen them on land. The stars above look like holes punctured into the sky, some other reality leaking through. Out on the beach, one lantern rises, its flame flickering, and in a rush, all the others follow. Without their lights close to him, the funeral procession vanishes into shadow, melting away and Morgan's eyes follow the lanterns' soft amber glow up into the sky.

"There's something else, Morgan, something important I've wrestled with because I'm not sure your mother wanted me to say anything…"

The old man turns to face him, the gold light of lanterns illuminating one side of his face and reflecting in his black eyes. Morgan wants it to be true, but even before Solomon speaks again, he's unsure, he can't believe it.

"Me and Dolores, we had a thing, briefly. I think, I'm pretty sure: you're my lad." As he speaks, his gaze moves to the horizon, though the boat does not need steadying.

"I know," says Morgan, squeezing his shoulder, "I mean, look at us. I must be." Sol's shoulder is hard with muscle, but the ageing skin loose. Morgan considers a hug, but it doesn't feel right. Maybe in time. The calm, grizzled man at the tiller of the boat is a good father, steady and in tune with the seasons of the sea, obviously adored by his daughter, Claire, warm beneath the gruffness. Morgan's breath is catching in his throat. This moment should be cathartic, a relief.

"I'm glad," says Solomon. "I saw you most summers when you were small, watched you grow up. I knew, and I hope I was kind to you. I'm only sorry I've not seen you much in recent years."

Morgan wants a deep sigh to come, or tears, or a roaring scream. But his body remains strung tight, like a violin string. He cannot help thinking: if he is Solomon's son, his mother would have told him; she would have no reason not to. But he smiles broadly at Solomon anyway.

"I'll leave you to tell Claire," says Sol. "I think it might be better coming from you to learn she has a brother."

Morgan takes a handful of ash, like coarse sand, or grey snowflakes, into his palms and empties them over the side. Then he offers the urn to Solomon, who takes it wordlessly and briskly sends Dolores out onto the breeze. Neither man speaks for a long time, then Solomon narrows his eyes and says, "The waves are getting up out there; I think the sea will be choppy tomorrow. We'd best head back."

Everyone is still out on the beach, though the darkness made Morgan think they had gone home. They are waiting for the boat to return. Claire loops her arm into his, and into her father's.

"You'll sleep well tonight," she says to both. And then to Morgan, "Before I forget – the photos you asked for." She hands him an A5 envelope. "I didn't look at them."

Morgan knows they could hold images, or simply the dark shadows that the light has spilled on them.

"Thank you." He says this to her, to Solomon, and to the Headland itself.

Monday 11th January 1988. After work (4.30 p.m.)

A cold fox, right outside the front window, just sitting, looking at me with amber eyes. Bright, bristling fur like a fire burning against the grey shingle and the grey sea.

I am very worried about Violet. It is too cold for her. There was a smattering of snow yesterday, soft feathers of it falling and heaping up on the windowpanes. She copied its feathery shapes on her face, but in black, as if in negative. Their images floated across her like static. Sometimes a plaintive, low hum emits from her body. I feel it through my feet, on my skin. She seems to be shrinking, at the same time her outline becoming clear as though she is fixing and will no longer be able to transform. I sat down to paint her at the weekend, as I often do, whilst softly chatting to her and feeding her newspapers. I found that I could see parts of her easily, that I could copy distinct lines of her form. I could represent her. A little insect-like, a little squid-like, but more definite, less mutable. This particular painting terrified me. This painting told me she is dying.

I piled log after log onto the fire. I ran a scalding bath for her, but she was not interested. I try to warm her but still her outline hardens for hours at a time. Then, with relief I see her soften and morph and pulse for ten or twenty minutes. Then the definite lines return. Images of the sound mirrors flicker across her face, then the yellow windows of Watchbell House, or the sea mine. Then nothing but shifting purple clouds. Only her face remains in constant flux, and the hardening of her body creeps towards it. I feed Wotsit, who is supple and warm. He rests his head on my lap. It's only a matter of time for Violet. I must love her with all my might until she leaves me. Perhaps her kind have a limited life span, or perhaps the environment here simply can't sustain her. I feel it is my fault.

The nights are dark and frozen and sometimes the wind cracks around the timbers of the house. I stay in my bed longer than usual in the mornings and retreat there early at night.

Morgan slept deeply the night of the funeral, as Claire said he would. He read a snippet of the diary until late and fell asleep with it open in his hand.

He has arranged to meet Solomon and Claire at Café Ferdinand. Randy is there too, not working but sitting on the veranda in the sun, white hair piled high, a mug in her hand. The wind is blowing around her, but she doesn't mind and stares out to sea at the gathering waves. Claire sits next to Morgan, drinking pink lemonade and twizzling the straw. He glances above her at his mother's sketches, even more enigmatic in the daylight, their lines and colours seeming to move and shift as he looks at them.

"It's a clever optical illusion, isn't it?" says Claire, reading his thoughts. "I haven't worked out how she did it. Your mother was so talented." Morgan agrees, realising he hasn't acknowledged this fully before. His mother was not simply his mother, but an artist, a maker, someone who wanted to show others her version of reality. The weird body of Violet brought this out. Dolores's attempts to capture a mutable creature led to these paintings: her attempts to know the wholly other.

Solomon walks in, the door jangling. He looks first at Morgan and offers a soft, shy smile. How strange if this is his father. Morgan's breath catches. "Can I order something for you, Solomon?" he says, an excuse to rise from his seat.

"Ah, sure. I'll have a beer. Just, you know, something cold and wet." He reaches across to his daughter's hand and squeezes it in easy greeting.

"It's table service," says the waitress, coming from behind the counter.

"I know," says Morgan, "I just…"

"Sorry if I kept you waiting."

"You didn't." His face reddens. He orders and goes back to the table, his heart beginning to settle. Solomon and Claire are talking. He listens, trying to be calm, trying to gauge what to say.

"Morgan and I had a good chat on the boat last night," says Solomon, eyeing Morgan from beneath his brows.

"We did," says Morgan, his voice a whisper. "It was good to catch up, to…to talk about Mum." He realises Solomon is giving him a chance to tell Claire, but he can't do it. He still isn't sure. He's overwhelmed by the idea that it might be true, and if it is, he has come home.

The wind gives a sudden moan outside, so loud that Solomon twists in his seat, and they watch Randy bluster back inside.

"It's getting up out there," she says.

"I'm betting on a storm tomorrow," says Solomon. "I feel it in my skin."

"You'd know. Sometimes I think you came out of the sea."

There is a silence. Claire smiles at Morgan over the rim of her glass.

"Been meaning to ask you, Claire, how's the new exhibition going?" says Solomon.

Claire grins. "Morgan doesn't know about it."

Morgan leans forwards. "Do tell me."

"It's a special exhibition for refugees. To raise awareness. Raise some money." She rummages in her rucksack and pulls out a black-and-white flyer. A woodblock print of a boat coming into the shore, crammed with silhouettes. A crowd is gathered there to meet them. *Art for Refugees: A Summer Exhibition: Squid Studio & Gallery*. Morgan shifts in his chair. Solomon, seeing his discomfort, says, "Claire might have told you: this is a spot for seekers coming in on boats. We're so close to France and it's one of the narrowest points. We help from time to time. People don't realise the waves are most dangerous near the shoreline. When I was living here, I'd take the boat out and help them in."

"It's just," joins Claire, "a lot of people are hostile. I want to show the refugees' side of the story. Their faces. Their tiny boats, unfit for the sea. A few local artists are involved."

She passes the flyer to Morgan, and he takes it, folds it in half and puts in carefully in his jacket pocket. He looks at them both, and a memory comes, unbidden, of a summer messing around in the sea, sun heating the shingle. Bright, calm water. He has never seen a refugee.

"Why come?" he asks. "If it's so dangerous? Why risk your life?"

Solomon clears his throat. "We don't want to judge. We dry them off, give them a hot drink, let the authorities take them somewhere safe. I know the sea, that's all. I know its lack of mercy."

Solomon is careful and measured, sipping his drink, but Morgan notices a flush painting Claire's cheeks.

"It's not that simple," she says. "Imagine you could be imprisoned or executed for talking or writing about something you believe in. Or your country is so economically depressed you can't feed your kids. It's about what kind of death you choose, what kind of risk."

Why would anyone launch themselves into that dark, unforgiving sea, even though it can be deceptively calm? There must be something far worse to escape from. But he is also possessive of this shingled, tufted landscape as though it is the only thing left of his mother. As if he had entered one of her paintings. *She* would never turn anyone away; there are no boundaries around Watchbell House.

"I like the idea of the exhibition," says Randy. "Sorry, I was being nosy." Her presence breaks the tension in the conversation. Solomon and Claire glance up at her at the same time with the same half smile and Morgan notices how alike their faces are. It could be their genes, or years of unconsciously mimicking each other's expressions. There is a wild light in their dark eyes, both have that untameable hair and a stubborn set to their shoulders. They are both fierce and beautiful, but, he thinks, not like him. And neither has his height; he towers above them both as he towered above his mother. He is a sail or a cloud or a tree.

The wind pushes against the windows and whips the striped awning on the veranda.

"I better go," says Solomon. "Secure the boat I'm borrowing." He rises and puts his hands on Morgan's shoulders. "Can we meet again tomorrow, lad, for a quick coffee? I've a few things I want to talk over with you."

"Of course."

"Oh, how mysterious," says Claire. She rises and puts her arms around her father's neck, smacks a kiss against his cheek. "Love you. It's nice to have you here for a bit."

His face crinkles into a broad grin. "Daft you are," he says, and the door jangles behind him.

Wednesday 13th January 1988. Late.

A sudden shift this evening. Almost impossible to explain. Even now, a wailing like a siren, like someone who can never be consoled, like the wind through the broken-down machinery on the shore. She is so loud, and it is otherwise so dark and silent outside, I wonder if anyone will hear and come. Then I will have to tell. Then they will get to her first. Let her be. Let her make that racket if she wants to protest her leaving this world. What will I do? What can I do?

A great flash of indigo light in the fire, enough to illuminate the whole house and make me cover my eyes. The front door is propped wide open, but she makes no move to go out.

I take it back; I can't stand her screaming anymore. I throw paper at her and leave bowls of water everywhere on the floors of Watchbell House. The walls vibrate. Wotsit has long fled into the night.

When will she stop?

Wednesday 20th January 1988.

It's over now. I can only just bring myself to write. I feel something heavy is settling on my chest and it will languish there forever, making my breath shallow and laboured. You know I have had this feeling before.

After that terrible night, Violet stopped wailing. She spread herself across the ceiling, pulsating and mutable again for a time. Calmed. She didn't want to go outside, no images flashed across her.

"I want to help you," I said, knowing she probably couldn't understand me. "Tell me how." I sat on the sofa and stared up at her, as if she were a cloud in the Headland sky, the roil of her iridescence like petrol moving in rainwater. Tears came and I let them roll down my cheeks, cool in the over-heated house. Soon that turned into sobbing. I was help-less. It was so late, and I was so tired. I closed Watchbell's door and crawled into bed, resolving to tell someone the next day, Randy or Solomon, in the hope that they would not think me mad. In the hope that Violet would be in her fixed form so that someone else could see her too. For too long I have coped with this alone. Too ~~proud, selfish, afraid,~~ distrustful to ask for help. No faith in others. Whatever the reason, I would tell someone for Violet's sake.

But things changed, and as it happens there is no need now to involve others. She is gone.

It happened like this: I fell asleep, exhausted by my tears and resolutions. Very late, perhaps in the early hours, I felt vibrations humming through the floorboards, and as I looked into the darkness of my bedroom, I saw Violet puls-ing towards me, flickering like a moonstone, bigger than I had ever seen her. Her legs, hundreds of them, flashed Prussian Blue and Rose Madder. Across her huge face rolled a shifting landscape of starlings and clouds; rain and damselflies; cats and seakale; scoping lighthouse beams and sound mirrors: everything she had ever encountered in every colour. And my face again, appearing before me like a self-portrait as she drifted, then oozed closer from the foot of my bed. Other faces too: Adrian with his beautiful, scarred lip; Solomon's dark curls and cormorant eyes; your gorgeous face, and another face, with a shock of hair, young, unrecognisable to me but also familiar as a dream.

Violet slid under the woollen blanket and along my skin and I felt her like tiny bolts of electricity, all my nerves prickling. She was warm like bathwater, fizzing and vibrating, but heavy, so heavy I couldn't move. My breath came in shudders as she spread herself across my torso. Some of her was wrapped around my skin, but some of her I felt inside me, amongst my organs, around my heart, deep within my abdomen. My lungs felt as though they were filling with water and she would drown me, but somehow my shuddering breaths gave me clear oxygen and my mind was sharp. I was terrified, but at the same time, I wanted her to stay with me there. I felt time oscillating, not moving forwards but forming a web that held me. Anything might happen. Everything might change, even things I thought were over and done with. My fingertips dissolved into the sky, as if the timber roof had been lifted clean off and I could feel the stars, the distant galaxies, and they all turned around each other only because my heart pulsed and for no other reason...

Then I drifted away into sleep and woke alone, my skin damp under the woollen blankets, frost on the windows. I went downstairs, wrapped in an old jumper, afraid. Violet was there in the cold grate on a bed of ash. She looked like a sketch of herself. Every line of her form was fixed. She was small, only the size of a piece of paper, and utterly still. She was two-dimensional. Her face, like a four-leaf clover, held one image, the simple representation of my eye, golden green with a black pupil, that she'd made when I first encountered her. I lifted her from the grate. She was cold and light, like origami. I placed her on the oak table next to the crackled driftwood that had been her shelter. I sat for a long time staring at her.

Then I left the house and stalked along the shoreline, hat jammed down and hands deep in my pockets. Seb was walking towards me, his loping stride and slight stoop identifying him before I could make out his features.

"Dolores, good to see you." His cheeks were red in the cold wind.

I wasn't sure if I would be able to speak, but it surprises me how good most of us are at acting the part, even when we feel like dying.

"What brings you to this end of the beach?" I asked.

"Break from work. Been working in a room without windows today so –" He gestured to the broad horizon, low clouds and circling gulls. I said nothing but stared at the astonishing white tipping the grey waves which frilled and collapsed on themselves.

"Dolly, can I ask you…" he turned to me and dug the toe of his boot into the shingle. "Are you alright? I was out here the other day and…well I heard a noise from your house. A cry. I wasn't sure and I don't want to intrude, but I almost knocked on the door. It stopped so I didn't. There was a very bright light too.…Sol said you won't see him. He'd like to see you…He really…"

"You worry too much Seb," I cut in, voice absolutely steady. I wanted him to be the one unsure of reality, distrustful of his senses. "I saw a fox outside my house, and you know how they have that human-sounding cry; it's uncanny. As for the light: I moved the TV, so I suppose it now faces the window. They were showing *Poltergeist* again; I had it on when I was cooking dinner."

I saw he didn't believe me; his face twisted into a half smile. I said nothing about his brother; that is none of his business.

"Listen," he said, softly putting his gloved hand on my shoulder, "if you need anything, just say. And if there is anything wrong, anything I can help with, ask me. We must stick together on the Headland, look out for each other. That's how it's always been."

I smiled and lifted his big hand from my arm. "Of course."

He walked away, back towards the power plant, and I wandered the Headland for the rest of the day until the sky darkened and the plant glowed.

As I approached Watchbell House, my hands were numb, and snow had begun to tumble from the black sky. I hoped that Violet had softened again, even for a few minutes, and returned to me. But I had avoided home all day because I knew I would come back to what I had left: a two-dimensional being like a cold sketch where Violet used to be. Something you could put in a glass case and remember her by, but that would never again be warm and bright and shifting like a storm. I opened the door slowly and looked across at the table. What I had left this morning was no longer there. Instead a small, black, leathery shape was in its place. It was rectangular, curved at the edges with four tendrils coming from it, dense, dry and smooth, puckered in the corners, sealed like an empty parcel. Like an urn. I placed it on the windowsill in the light of the power station.

I wondered how I might continue my life. Wotsit mewed from the kitchen, bent over his empty food bowl.

Morgan is sitting on the porch of Watchbell House with hot, sweet coffee, and the envelope of photos. The diary has taken a turn, and he wants to see if there are clues in the images. He has arranged to meet Solomon in a couple of hours. He is rehearsing all of the questions he wants to ask about his mother's relationship with him. Why didn't they stay together? Why did she never mention him? He realises Solomon was always in his life, present in his childhood, but hovering at the edges like waves coming in and out on the shoreline. The hot weather has broken, and the day is grey, threatening a storm, and the waves are high, as Solomon predicted. The wind pushes through his hair, but he wants to be outside, after days of cloying weather.

Morgan sifts the photographs onto his lap. Monochrome images of Watchbell's garden, neater than it is now, flints and driftwood rising from the shingle, trimmed elder bushes and delicate roses, his mother, very young to Morgan's eyes, beaming in the background, gardening gloves on, leaning on a spade. She looks well fed, her cheeks puffed out with a grin, her hair tumbling down her back. Then there are photos of wrecked boats, their weathered wood and coating of barnacles; then the narrow-gauge train moving along the track with its puff of grey steam. There are some images of an unfamiliar cobbled street, again with his mother posing at the top of the hill. In a couple of the photographs a tall, fair-haired man offers a half smile, shading his eyes with his hand, or wades into the sea in the distance. Perhaps this is Adrian. Morgan saw no one like this at the funeral. He leafs through the photos quickly. The last three are of the interior of Watchbell House looking barely any different forty years ago. These photos are darker, more difficult to make out, no flash has been used and the natural light is minimal. One image shows the oak table under the window, a twisted piece of driftwood on its surface. Morgan holds the photo up to the light and squints. Maybe there is something there: a dusting of warped light, no colour of course, but a distortion, a shape. But then, no, it's nothing, just the table, the driftwood, the blurred outline of the power station beyond that.

Morgan looks up. He's never seen the waves so high; the wind is whining through the gaps between the cottages. In the next photograph: the kitchen worktop, perhaps there is an extra shadow and he cannot see what casts it…Suddenly the wind snatches the last photograph from Morgan's hand, the one he has not yet seen, and sends it spinning down the beach. He tries to sprint after it, feet sliding into the shingle. He loses sight of it as it is whipped into the coming storm, but he notices an orange boat out on the huge waves. Why would anyone go out when the sea is like this? It looks like only a dinghy, something inflatable and listing to the side, half-filled with water. As he nears the beach, Morgan hears snippets of voices shouting and sees people in the water, the bright colours of their clothes against the grey waves, disappearing and reappearing in the currents. He runs towards the shore.

Some of them are wading onto the beach being knocked back by the waves, others are already on the shore, shouting hoarsely. Some collapse onto the shingle. Then, farther down the shoreline he sees Claire leaning over something – a dark shape. It is so windy, and the rain has turned from drizzle to hard, straight lines, obscuring his vision. Claire is saying something, but the sudden thunder of the blades of a helicopter overhead means he cannot hear her. She rocks forwards, then back again. He stumbles over and stops before he reaches her, unable to take a further step.

"I told him not to go in," she says, leaning down, her knees sinking into the hard shingle. "I told him to wait for the coastguard, but he wouldn't listen."

Solomon's body lies on the beach, his clothes soaked and sticking to his wiry limbs, mouth slightly parted and trickling with water, eyes half-open. His arms are loosely wrapped around a tiny child who is face down on his chest, not moving. Claire strokes the wet, white curls away from her father's forehead. "I told him not to go in. I told him not to go in," she says, over and over. Morgan should look at the child, lift the body, check for a pulse, but he does nothing. The sky is dark and heaped with clouds. There is distant shouting behind him, and footsteps slipping on the crunching shingle, coming closer. A strong arm swings from the left and pushes him aside. He stumbles back. Another person runs in, heavy boots and green clothes, swinging a bag. They obscure the two bodies. The helicopter rumbles above. Someone leads Claire away – half drags her still repeating her phrase as if stuck in an endless loop of time.

Morgan steadies himself and looks behind him. A man is running towards them, another child in his arms, this one breathing and alive with his legs wrapped around the man's torso. The man is wailing, wailing. He pushes Morgan aside and to the ground with such force that Morgan is winded, a sharp stone cutting into his arm. The paramedic restrains the man, who lets the child he is carrying down to the ground. The paramedic raises her palms in the air and says, "Stay here; let us help him."

The child is standing only feet from Morgan. He might be four or five years old. His skin looks grey and his clothes are soaked. He splutters and coughs and stares up at his father, who moves towards the bodies of Solomon and his younger child, and then is clawing desperately at the paramedic's chest. The paramedic holds him until the man's body collapses to the ground; he has lost the will to stand. The tiny body of the child, smaller than his brother, is stretchered away, and the father is too weak to follow. He only wails, wails at the stormy sky and the helicopter still trying to help those in the water.

The boy standing on the beach turns and looks at Morgan, who is rising to his feet. He stares up at him as he stands, his deep brown eyes searching Morgan's face. He says something in a language Morgan doesn't understand. It sounds like a question. Morgan doesn't know how to answer, but he takes off his cardigan and drapes it across the boy's shoulders. It makes the boy look even smaller. Then someone puts their hand on the boy's back and leads him away.

Morgan is only an observer. Time swirls around him. Solomon's body lies motionless on the beach like a piece of driftwood; for a few moments whilst they bring a stretcher, nobody is with him. His muscles, tight from years of reeling in fish and hauling crab nets, are already relaxing into death, his body pushed back out by the sea he loved. Morgan was going to meet him for coffee to talk about his mother. All the questions Morgan was going to ask still clog his throat. He swallows them. He looks up the beach for Claire but cannot see her. More people from the boat are walking towards him. He looks at his hands, blood leaking from little cuts the shingle has made. Headlanders are running down the beach to help. Watchbell is in the distance with its overgrown garden. He must tend to that; his mother would not have wanted it to get out of hand. The yellow front door is still open, and he sees now that he's scattered the photographs all over the beach. Some are heading out to sea on the wind, some are being washed back by the furious waves. He leaves them and walks back towards the open door, the father still wailing behind him.

<u>Sunday 14th February 1988. Evening.</u>

I keep writing here, if only to remind myself that life is going on. Each morning I have my breakfast at the table, the driftwood and the leathery pouch beside me. I wonder sometimes how Violet could have been real. I spent the first few days after she'd gone just sleeping, keeping Wotsit fed and idly stroking him. I went to work and watched my students draw and paint. I vowed I would never stop painting because it was Violet who had helped me to break my block. Then one morning, I filled the bath, washed my hair and hoovered up the confetti of punched paper from the living room. I cleared out the grate, sprinkling the ashes on Watchbell's garden, which is coming back to life with a smattering of bowing snowdrops. I ate toast with butter and marmalade and a hot mug of tea. I tidied the kitchen. I went outside and drew the salt air into my lungs. I was sad and the sadness sat behind my eyes, damned up and wobbling, but I was still living.

Mum was on good form today; she knew me and hugged me tightly when I arrived.

"Look at the garden," she said, leading me to the conservatory. "It's coming back to life. There'll be spring flowers soon." I saw the little shoots of green poking through the frost. I brought scones this time and we ate them with butter and strong tea.

"You're sad, Dolly-mixture. You never liked the winter; summer babies never do. Your sister loves the rain because April is such a wet month. That's why she moved to Seattle."

I smiled. She says this often. I think I used to like the winter once, but the Headland does look bleak and haunted at this time. I have only lived here for two winters. The wind is biting, and the frilled sea, so lit up in summer, doesn't want us humans here now, it wants to sulk and darken in the cold. The sky is heavy with the threat of icy rain and the old lighthouse looks like the black stump of a bare tree. The gulls shiver and scream, the seakale is buffeted, and the viper's bugloss are dead sticks. It will all change soon though. I have seen it come back to life before.

Monday 22nd February 1988. Late.

Protestors at the plant. I went out to the nature reserve to walk the trail of hides, retracing my steps with Violet. Peering through the slats of the first hide, with a view of the power station, I saw a crowd moving and heard the far-off echo of a chant catching me only when the breeze carried a certain way over the lake. Mallards circling, looking cold, widgeons with their pretty green masks, whooper swans out standing on the banks, white in the pale reeds. There are binoculars to borrow in the hide, so I looked at the plant closely and saw perhaps twenty or so people at the plant's entrance. They had placards with slogans: *Nuclear Power Makes Mutants; Ban Radiation; We Are Not Safe.* Some carried nasty images of Chernobyl victims, both of the disaster and those born after. I've heard these protests happen from time to time, but never seen one. Two security guards stood by looking embarrassed, and then, as someone got close to a door, they moved them roughly and a tussle broke out, then subsided.

I returned from my walk around dusk. Watchbell House rose in the distance above the shingle and I saw three figures silhouetted at the door: Seb, Solomon and someone I didn't recognise. He was holding a small machine that looked like a Dictaphone.

"Hello," I said. Sol ran a hand through his curls. He smelled briny, come straight from a catch. Seb smiled.

"Hi, Dolores. This is Matthew, he's just come because there's been a concern about the radiation levels around here. It's very…routine for us to check on the cottages from time to time. Outside here we got a reading and…Do you mind if we come in and check?"

I couldn't understand what he meant, and I didn't have Violet to worry about anymore. As I had that thought and unlocked the door, my chest felt heavy and my arms tingled. There really was nothing to hide from them.

"That's a bit worrying," I said, letting them enter the house before me. "It's not as if I even go near the plant."

"It doesn't necessarily work like that," said Matthew, who was very blond, with acne around his jawline, but not young. He held the machine up and it clicked.

"Tea?" I said.

"Oh yes," Matthew answered, but at the same time Seb said, "No, we're not going to be long," and shot him a look. Matthew pursed his lips. The clicking got faster.

"Readings increase over here." I watched him walk over to the table. *Click. Click. Clickclickclick.* "Borderline reading here. He frowned, turning over the driftwood. "Strange. Where did you get this?"

"Just at the beach." My voice came out as a whisper. My heart, so sluggish, suddenly started to batter my ribcage. Matthew flipped a plastic bag out of his pocket, deftly, with one hand.

"What are you doing?"

"I've got to take this. It seems to be contaminated." He said it as if it was just rubbish.

"You can't. It's for my art. My projects." I was surprised by how desperate I sounded.

Matthew looked baffled and his eyes slid to Seb, who was frowning. Sol stood back, near the kitchen, and I caught his eye for a moment. It steadied me.

"When did you find it, Dolores?" asked Seb. "Was it after the storm, in October? It's important to know how long it's been in the house."

"I don't think so; later than that. I wanted it for a still life; a painting…" I trailed off because I knew he'd take it, and I knew it was just a broken shell where something I loved used to be. The bag crackled as he hauled it in. Sol avoided my gaze then and looked out of the window at the low, grey clouds.

"There's no immediate danger," said Matthew. "But we'll analyse it and come back if we're concerned."

"Thanks, Dolly," said Seb. He looked tired, I noticed then: his straight hair needed a cut, the skin around his eyes was grey. They turned to go. Sol looked at me again then and said, "I'll have one. A cuppa, I mean. Just a quick one. I'm frozen. It's mean out there on the sea today."

Seb nodded and closed the door behind him and Matthew. I put the kettle on the hob to boil, and before long, it began to shriek.

"A mermaid's purse," Sol said above the noise. I poured the tea, only half-listening.

"A what?" I turned around with the tea to see him holding what is left of Violet, gently in his palm; the strange, leathery remnant.

"It's called a mermaid's purse. Did you find it on one of your beach walks? They are unusual around this shore."

"I didn't know they had that name," I said, glad he had mistaken it for one of those.

"See these tendrils, they're designed to fasten to rocks. A bit like Velcro." He sipped his tea, steam curling around his lips.

"But what for?"

"Well," he smiled and, unbidden, put his arm around my waist with a light touch. I didn't move away from him. "Really, they are egg pouches where the young of rays or sharks develop. Occasionally I'll dislodge one by mistake with a net, and I've seen the half-grown rays, like shadows, moving inside. I try to put them back. Sometimes they wash up on the shore with life inside them, sometimes spent and dry like this one…A nice find." He placed it carefully back on the ledge. "Sorry about your driftwood, by the way; I'll try to find you another one."

At the word "another" I broke into sobs; what was shored up behind my eyes and at the back of my throat came out in a wash of salt and snot. I clung around Sol's neck, my head pushed against his shoulder so he couldn't see my face with all the control gone from it, ugly with grief. He put both arms around me and let it go over him until it stilled.

I asked him to stay with me. Not because I need to forget. Not because of that but because I am alive. Every bit of me is alive and so is every bit of Sol. He wanted to wash the smell of the catch off his body. I told him not to; I wanted the real stench of the sea, too much and acrid with brine, the sex smell of crustaceans and seaweed. Mackerel scales, like tiny mirrors, transferred from Sol's fingertips to my skin, sparkling in the intermittent light that broke through the clouds and into the windows of Watchbell House.

Morgan reads his mother's journal all afternoon, sipping whisky from a dusty bottle he finds tucked behind the fireplace. He wonders why he is still reading it but doesn't want to be left with his own thoughts. He can't stop seeing Solomon's pale body, the child across his chest, lying on the shingle. Or Claire's bewildered expression, her hands busy with pushing the curls back from her father's forehead. But it is the man and his other son, the boy's eyes searching his own, that will never fade. Sometime in the early evening, the police come to Watchbell House to ask him questions. One is young, a man with a delicate, hairless face; the other a woman in her fifties like Claire, poised and calm, a lifetime of accumulated moments like this behind her steady eyes. He feels ashamed as he tells them what happened, feels that he should have helped. They seem satisfied with his account. After they leave, he goes up to the bedroom, gets into the creaking bed fully clothed and stares at the shadows gathering in the corner of the ceiling. Then he drifts, impossibly, into sleep.

The next day is bright and blue and cloudless, as if nothing has happened. He decides to avoid the beach; he can see yellow tape and groups of officials and police in the distance. He cannot think what he would say to Claire, or Randy, or anyone. He walks instead along the perimeter of the power station, comforted by the hum of the pylons and the idea that inside, people are busy with gauges and machinery. He passes along the track, past the well-kept bungalows and through the gate to the lake. Then over the gravel path in the cool shade of the tall hedges that buzz with goldfinches and vibrate with the tiny engines of damselflies. Swans drift on the lake with mallards and coots, and a fan of swallows rises.

Morgan continues to the locked swing bridge and the concrete domes of the sound mirrors. His mother used to walk with him here in summers and he'd lean on the bridge and imagine them as alien craft, landed and broken open like huge eggs, or futuristic castles for robots to wage war on one another. The large, curved one is flocked with gulls; when they see him, they rise and shriek, but they come back down and settle again. It was here, as he got older, that he told his mum he wanted to study history. He was so fascinated by the idea that the sound mirrors were created as a warning system for enemy ships and aircraft, huge stethoscopes designed to listen to the coast's chest, but that almost the moment they were finished, the invention of radar made them obsolete. How strange and beautiful and useless they are. But it is only time that made them so.

He rests against the gate and takes out his phone.

"Maggie," he says.

"Morgan! Are you alright? How was the funeral and everything? I didn't want to hassle you…" Her voice is sleepy, as though she's woken from a nap. Morgan pictures her propped in bed, the soft curve of her belly, rubbing sleep from her green eyes.

"I…How are you? How's the baby?"

"Fine, fine. I'm starting to waddle now. A bit tired. But it's not going to be long. He or she is wriggling away."

Morgan thinks of the two little boys on the beach, soaked in cold saltwater, one face down on Solomon's chest, the other asking him a question he cannot fathom.

"And work, tell me about that."

"Morgan, really; you don't need to ask," Maggie says softly. "It's okay."

"No, no; I'm interested. I want to know. It's…a bit isolated here; I like to hear what you're up to."

"Well, we're looking again at the relationship between heat and time. Thermodynamics, you know…How heat only moves one way from warm to cooler, and so time only appears to move one way – past to future. But…but the weird part is that's only because of probability. So, the movement of heat is why we perceive time as linear. It's another head fuck, Morgan." Her words come out in a rush, as if from another world that Morgan left not a few days but decades ago. He doesn't understand her but makes an affirmative grunt as if he does. He has been rehearsing his breakup speech, his cowardly way of getting out by saying he can't be a father. But he was going to phrase it so that she knows she's better off without him. He was going to be unkind so she would hate him and want him gone. But now, everything has changed.

"But Morgan, you sound…Do you need to talk? No pressure," Maggie says brightly.

"Yeah; I think I do. Something happened. Something else. I'm not sure what to do…"

He tells her about Solomon. As he speaks, he realises he's rarely talked about his emotions with Maggie. He hasn't allowed her to know his feelings, but has instead sought solace in her skin, the push of her lips and tongue, the grip of her legs and arms around him. What would she have to say about death? What would she know about it?

"Oh, Morgan," she says, breathing into the phone, "this is so terrible. Do you want me to come there? I can come."

All at once, he longs for her to come. He has been trying to break away from her, planning his escape route, but he wants nothing more than for her to be there at the door of Watchbell House, with her arms open, even as the curve of the baby bulges between them.

"No," he says. "Don't come. Stay and rest. The baby is coming soon. It won't be comfortable for you to travel."

"Okay. But come home soon. I don't want you dealing with this by yourself."

Neither of them speaks for a moment. But he knows she is there. The city whirrs behind her in the background, loud with sirens and voices and wheels.

"I'm not even sure if he was my dad," says Morgan. "I don't even know. Why didn't Mum tell me?"

"She must have had a good reason," says Maggie. Maybe this is one thing she understands well that he doesn't. "It's going to be okay," she says softly. "In time."

She's been trying to tell him time isn't what he thinks it is. But right now, it feels like there is no other way of thinking about it: Solomon is gone, gone in this point in time, never to be met again, his breath replaced by saltwater. For the first time, though, Morgan sees his baby as a person that, if he chooses to, he will meet. A baby suspended, waiting, who will soon belong to time. A baby who will grow to be a child, and may stand before him on the beach, shading their eyes with their small hands.

After the call, Morgan tracks back around the lake. He is thinking about Maggie, her kind words about the refugees, how she told him none of this is his fault or ever could be, that it must be so hard to have lost Solomon. Shame thickens in his chest and clogs his throat. He hears the chants of the protestors at the power station, their voices carried on the sea breeze. He follows the shingled path so automatically that he takes a wrong turn on the way back, and he's at the edge of the plant, walking past the small gathering. They aren't aggressive, but the group jostle and bump against him, their voices merging, knocking him accidentally with their placards.

"Keep clean power. Don't close the plant," they sing.

Morgan's ears are humming, and his head feels loose, like it might float away. The sky darkens. The placards read: *Save Our Power Station* and *Keep Zero Emission Energy*, but as he looks up at them, jerking in the hands of the protestors, he notices other signs that say: *Close the Power Station: Radiation Kills*. The crowd multiplies, and Morgan is caught inside them – someone closes the circle. There were only about ten people, now there seems to be fifty or more. He can smell their sweat. "Radiation kills. Keep clean energy," they chant. It doesn't make sense: they can't be in favour of *and* against the plant. One of his episodes is coming on, he can feel it. He needs to sit down. His knees are giving way. But the crowd might crush him if he isn't standing. The corner of a placard thrusts out and catches him on the eye socket. He crumples.

He wakes in the early evening, a chill prickling his skin, a clutch of swallows twisting overhead. His eye is sore, a little bruised, but other than that he is unharmed. The power station looms above him, its angular shadow against the darkening sky. He hears someone clear their throat, sits up and sees their silhouette, sitting by the scrubby bushes next to the station. The man is angular, thin, deeply tanned, his grey hair pulled into a bun. He is staring at Morgan.

"Are you alright?" he asks, in a voice unexpectedly refined.

"Yes, I think so," says Morgan. The man rises, as if to leave. There is nobody else here.

"I said I'd hang back, until you woke up. Can I take you back to your home?"

"No, no it's alright, it's only…" Morgan gestures to the beach. He stands up, rubs his eye. "I'm fine."

The man brushes the grit from his hands. "I'll join the others in the pub then."

"Before you go," says Morgan, "I just wondered: why did I see signs for *and* against the plant being open?"

The man frowns, deep lines between his brows and around his eyes. "You won't have," he says. "We are in support of the plant remaining open. Despite the risks, nuclear is the only way to go. Carbon neutral theoretically. Back in the day, of course, people were very afraid of an accident, a meltdown. But now, well you know, we've got to stop using fossil fuels, burning the planet we live on."

Morgan thinks of the placards he saw, the muddle of messages. "I must have been mistaken. There aren't two groups of you or anything? Opposing groups?"

"Nope, just us, trying to keep it open. Government needs to fund the upkeep, modernise the tech. Spending all our taxes on defence, vaccines, trade agreements. Don't know their arses from their elbows on most matters. Pardon my French." He gestures away to the horizon, as if to apologise to France itself.

They both smile. The man gives a little salute and tracks back around the perimeter of the plant. Morgan walks slowly back towards the beach. He knows both messages were there, somehow: protestors from the past meeting protestors from the present. Two timelines impossibly coming together. As if time had folded, just for a moment, back on itself.

<u>Tuesday 8th March 1988, 6 p.m.</u>

I'm tending Watchbell's garden, which has started to thrive
again. Wotsit stalks around on the shingle, looking for
lizards which like to bask on the larger stones. Today was
warm for March; a soft breeze came off the sea. Boats were
sliding through the waves, people walking on the shoreline. I sowed packets of seeds that I got from Gold Stone,
poppy and sweet pea, and tried to protect the fennel with
netting; rabbits eat it all in spring and summer. The cro-
cuses are out: bright oranges and yellows against the grey
flints, and the dog roses, a little scorched from high winds
a few days ago. A tranquil day with the feeling that summer is not far away. The beach will soon be filled with bird
watchers and tourists, Randy's café full of their chatter. I
took up my easel and sat with it on the porch, looking to
the hazy horizon, and painted the shifting sky. I'm thinking of a triptych: sky and sea; power station; and my own
ink-black house, glowing as the sun goes down.

<u>Monday 14th March 1988, 9.30 p.m.</u>

The windows stream with rain, no view of anything
through them. I struggled to get to work today with the
wind stinging my face all the way to the bus stop. Then my
students were out of sorts because there was no chance at
all of going outside.

"Let's paint the rain and the way the rain changes things,"
I said. An artist always tries to turn the situation into

inspiration; it's how we get through times that are not as we would hope. I had a treat for them too: fresh squid ink, a new medium to work with. But they hated its sexual stink and the way it stained their fingers. Except for Claire. She used it to sketch a beautiful rain-streaked tree that looked like it was dissolving into the sky.

When I returned, a man was waiting for me, sheltered under the porch. He had on a dark suit and was tall and thin with a lugubrious face. I thought of undertakers. His hair was very wet and slicked back from his square fore-head. He smelled of damp wool and tobacco.

"Apologies, Mrs Poole," he said. "I've come from the plant. My name is Clement." He didn't clarify if this was a first name or surname. I invited him in, and he sat on the sofa, legs awkwardly bent, with a coffee steaming in his hands. He glanced with distaste around my little house, as if he might catch a disease if he touched anything.

"The log that you gave us for analysis…"

"You mean the driftwood?"

"Err, yes. Okay. Well, I've just come to reassure you."

I stood by the cold fireplace; I thought if I sat down, he might stay for longer. He told me that the radiation levels were unusually high for something like wood, but not harmful so long as I had not been exposed for many years. But they had also found traces of three other chemicals, two banned in this country and one chemical they had not been able to identify.

"Perhaps because of how old the wood is, we could not match that to any known substance." As he said this, he frowned as though he would always be troubled by it. He suspected the wood had washed up after many years at sea, having originated in another country, perhaps contaminated by its proximity to a factory, when it was still living, absorbing the chemicals from the soil and air around it. I wondered if Violet had lived in the tree whilst it was alive and breathing and had travelled with it or had found it later. He thanked me for letting him take it.

"We believe you are safe," he added. "But if you experience any symptoms, please contact your doctor and then me." He gave me his card and a sheet of paper with a printed list. After he'd gone, back out into the pouring rain which closed like a curtain around his shoulders, I read the list: *Headache; Burning sensation; Skin rash; Itching; Hair loss; Sudden weight loss; Loss of appetite; Erectile dysfunction; Irregular menstrual cycle; Hallucinations; Paranoia; Lethargy; Cramps; Diarrhoea; Visual disturbances or impairment; Hearing disturbance or loss; Nosebleeds; Unexplained cough; Shortness of breath; Insomnia; Heart palpitations…*

The list went on and on and didn't distinguish between male and female bodies. I screwed it up and put it into the grate with a little pyramid of kindling, then lit it. The flames rose blue and cobalt green, and I watched it curl and disappear.

<u>Thursday 31st March/Friday 1st April 1988. Late/Early.</u>

I've just woken up. I'm in bed, covers pulled up, writing beneath them. I feel hot and sweaty, but also oddly cold. The reason I'm awake: a new sound all around me.

Flapping. Fluttering.

Something must be batting against the windowpanes. But it is also in the walls. The moon is bright; I cannot see anything out there but the deep grey, sliding clouds. The flapping continues like a beached fish landed improbably on the floorboards.

It's a delicate sound, a brushing against wood, a heart tremor. I turn the light on. Shadows and highlights but no movement. The corners of my unfinished canvases leaning against the wall. I wonder if the fluttering is inside my ear, as if some tiny creature is struggling against my eardrum. My skin prickles.

Nothing. Nothing.

I will sleep downstairs; I can't stand it.

<u>Easter Sunday, 3rd April 1988. About 4 p.m.</u>

I told Mum about my week over our lamb and mint sauce. She asked me to pick all the mint pieces out. Today she seemed childlike and clumsy with her cutlery. She peered at me over some knitting full of dropped stitches, as if there were fog over her eyes.

I said, "A thrush, a baby one, flew through the open window and crashed into the wall." She couldn't remember what a thrush was, so I told her: a songbird with a speckled breast and a chittering, cheerful song. This one was a fat chick, with his adult feathers coming in, round like a bun and dazed. Wotsit eyed him but didn't go for him. I cupped the chick in my hands, hot as pastry, silky wings and sharp claws, and the thrum of a tiny heart behind his breast. I took him into the garden. He was still there the day after but gone the next. A spot of blood on the wall above the fireplace. I didn't wipe it away.

I thought he might have been the source of the fluttering, but I still hear it at night, so I have taken to sleeping downstairs again with Wotsit warming my feet. I feel haunted, but I know you wouldn't try to terrify me.

Solomon will come later to look in the attic. I told him about the noises, worried that he might think me mad. But he just narrowed his eyes and said he would investigate, as if he has an idea of what it might be. I am too afraid to pull down the creaky ladder and do it myself, not because of what he might find, but because there may be nothing there at all.

Thursday 7th April 1988. Early morning.

Solomon climbed the ladder whilst I waited at the bottom. He took the torch and I watched him disappear into the blackness of the loft space. The beam of light swung around; I could just make it out through the hatch's square of dark. Silence.

Then he said, "You should come up here, Dolores. I can see what you have here."

My heart thrummed in my chest like the little thrush's. But it was something Sol could see too, so I decided it was okay to go up, the ladder creaking under my feet. I don't like heights, so I crawled from the hatch into the loft and stayed on my knees. It was pitch-black but for the beam of light Sol pointed into the upper corner of the eaves. Sol's face was half-lit, half-invisible. There was a yeasty smell, the scent of crumbling tar, an undertone of dried shit. At first, I saw nothing. Then I made out a cluster of shapes high up in Watchbell's roof structure, folded in on themselves, faces like furred insects or mice, flared nostrils and leathery skin. Bats. Six or seven of them, trembling slightly, eyes shining in our light, one flexing a wing to show the translucent skin. My own skin flashed hot for a moment and tears came up and sat behind my eyes; I was both relieved and disappointed.

"It's a bit of a problem," said Sol, "these are Horseshoe Bats. Protected species; difficult to move."

I thought of watching them flying out at dusk using their clicking echolocation to navigate. I thought of them folded up there above my head.

"It's okay," I told Sol. "I don't mind them, now I know what they are. We can leave them be."

"They won't do any harm," he said.

We climbed down, Sol closing the hatch with a dusty clatter. He went back to his fishing boat, and I spent the rest of the day amongst the gorse now thriving in the garden. When night came, I saw the bats swooping around in the indigo light. I must have mistaken them for birds, or else not been looking at all, not realising what was there all the time.

You see, I suppose, only what you want to see.

Morgan is in Watchbell's garden, furiously pulling up weeds and trimming roses. His hands are bare and already bloody with cuts. His mother would not have wanted the garden to be overgrown and untidy, and the summer has allowed the weeds to thrive and the plants to overspill their boundaries. He's uncovered a flint stick, rising from the shingle with *Wotsit* etched onto it. The big orange cat he used to tease. He thinks of Wotsit's buried bones, roots tangled around them. He knows nothing about cultivating things, having only watched his mother, and grown a sad basil plant on his city flat's balcony. He's sweating and piling up the cuttings, so engrossed in his task he does not see Randy coming up Watchbell's path towards him until she is almost there.

"Morgan, I didn't take you for a gardener. When you were little, you always played on the beach or sat with your colouring books whilst your mother did this."

Morgan stops to look at Randy, who is not wearing her usual glamorous makeup, and whose hair is over-spilling from its pins. The wind ruffles her blouse and she looks thin beneath it.

"Randy – I…I'm so sorry about Solomon."

Randy sighs and folds her arms across her torso. "Well, you know, he died in the sea, which was his favourite place to be." She looks towards the horizon, as if she might still see Solomon there on the waves, out in his boat. "I don't know who's going to scatter his ashes on the water…I suppose there are plenty of people with boats here," she says, more to herself than to Morgan. "Listen, I came because Claire wants to see you."

Morgan's stomach twists. He knows he must face Claire. He nods.

"Let me just wash my hands, lock up."

A few minutes later he follows Randy along the beach, up the sandy dunes tufted with grass, and into Café Ferdinand. Claire is in a booth near the window, a coffee cup steaming in her hands. Morgan sits opposite her. Her eyes are puffy, but she smiles softly at him. Morgan touches one of her fingers lightly, where it curls around the cup. Randy brings him a coffee too, laced with something warm and strong.

"I'm so sorry, Claire."

She nods, bites her lip.

"At least," she says, voice delicate and vibrating, "at least he did some good before he died, saving that little boy."

"But I thought the boy was…"

Claire shakes her head once. "So did I. But apparently, they revived him at the scene and he's stable in the hospital now. Little kids can go much longer without oxygen. He's going to be alright."

Morgan's breath turns ragged in his throat. He hears the wailing of the father again in his ears, sees the brother staring up at him and asking his question, wearing Morgan's cardigan over his small shoulders. The child is going to be alright. He's going to be alright. The walls of the café lurch. He sips the coffee, grateful for whatever Randy has added to it. For a while, they sit in silence, looking out at the grass on the dunes which tugs and drifts against the breeze, the grey-blue sea and the tourists wandering the beach. The café is half-full, and Morgan is grateful for the low chatter of the other tables, softening the edges of his own voice.

"Claire," he says. "Your father and my mum. Were they close?"

She looks up, brightens. "They seemed to be good friends. My dad left the Headland when I was a teenager, went to the city with his brother, Sebastian. The city didn't suit him much, I don't think, though…No horizon, no sea. He came back often to see me and spent a few weeks here every summer. I'm pretty sure he took you with us on fishing trips from time to time…But when I went off to art school and got older, he came less. He got a job fishing up North. He liked the cold and the cleaner water of the North Sea. He always said the fish were better."

"So, he never came back permanently to the Headland?"

Claire sips her coffee for the first time, blinking at the alcohol it is laced with. "Gosh, Randy knows how to treat us, doesn't she?" She allows herself a smile. "No, he didn't come back to live, only to visit. Uncle Seb said something happened at the Headland that disturbed him, though I never found out what."

Morgan shifts in his seat and gazes out of the window again. He imagines the meeting he and Solomon were going to have a few days ago. He studies Claire's face, looking for similarities to his own. He wants to tell her but feels he can't do that now: she has no idea. "And your uncle Seb?" he ventures.

"He died a few years ago. He was very happy in London – had kids and everything. But his health wasn't great in his seventies. I visit my cousins quite a lot. It's an excuse to see the amazing galleries too."

Morgan walks Claire back to her studio. She takes his arm and it comforts them both. But when they get there, the three men Morgan encountered on the beach, and a number of others, are crowding around the studio door. Morgan spots Ashlie from the Hope and Anchor amid the crowd, but she does not acknowledge him. Claire leans closer to Morgan and tightens her grip on his arm.

"What do you want?" she says, unlocking the door as the leader of the group moves aside.

"Just to look at the art," he says, louder than he needs to. "It says on the door you're open at this time."

"Well, I've been a bit tied up."

She steps in. Morgan follows her and gives her a quizzical look. She returns it with a light shake of her head. The group step in, crowding the small gallery, obscuring the light and shadows of the paintings. One takes a painting of a fishing boat off the wall to look at it.

"You don't need to do that," says Claire, putting her keys on the counter. "Just ask me about them, and if you want to buy one, I'll get one from out back. Those are display only."

"Oh, okay," says the mucous-voiced man, smiling. He drops the picture to the floor and the glass in the frame cracks. Claire sighs and Morgan hears a sob rising in her throat.

"Listen," Morgan says, "there is no need to cause trouble here. You know what happened a few days ago. It's been really difficult for the Headlanders. You need to lay off."

"Well, that's why we're here. We heard a local died because of those illegals. We think it's high time this stopped." Directly to Claire he says, "People like you, helping those immigrants, you're to blame for this." He shoves a crumpled flyer for the refugee exhibition against Morgan's chest.

"Now steady on," says Morgan. There are seven of them standing in the gallery in front of him, their eyes and faces blurring into one like a sea monster.

"We mean it," says another. "This is what happens when you let foreigners come in. Money spent on our coastguard, our doctors. One of our own dying."

"He's not one of yours!" screams Claire from the corner of the gallery. "He's mine, my father. How dare you. Get out of here."

The seven pairs of eyes look surprised for a moment, then they back out of the door, muttering, the smell of their sweat lingering in the air long after they have left. Morgan watches them kicking and stomping down the beach. They congregate by the old sea mine, leaning against its barnacled and rusted dome, glancing back at the studio from time to time.

"Don't let them in here again, Claire. Ban them."

"Then I'm just as bad, aren't I?" she says mechanically, picking up the broken picture.

Saturday 30th April 1988, 7.45 p.m.

I learn to live without her, Violet, my strange friend. I
don't know what she was or why she visited me, or why
she went after such a short time. She was never easy to see,
and now when I try to picture her, I barely can. I see only
the hard, two-dimensional form like an ink drawing that
she became just before she left me with the leathery pouch
Solomon calls a mermaid's purse. I miss talking to her,
softly chatting about nothing at all. I miss her proboscis
vaporising dishes of water, her glowing in the grate, the
images moving across her face like storm clouds. I think
of the shuddering weirdness of her touch and what she
showed me of the universe before she dried up and left me
with a husk of herself.

Sol spends more time here. He doesn't talk a lot. He likes
to cook, filling my kitchen with fresh scents, or wash up, or
fix a cracked window or lolling shelf. I don't encourage him
to come. I feel comfortable in my aloneness, but I don't
turn him away either.

Now the summer is approaching, the garden keeps me
busy with weeding. Deep green broom is coming up, and
mallow and white campion. The viper's bugloss are bright
purple and scattered all over the beach. I walk there most
days and smell the honey breath of the seakale and the salt
coming off the water. The beach is busier: tourists climb
over the old sea mine and photograph the wrecked boats.

Some dare to go into the sea, which won't warm up until August. As summer nears, I find memories of my childhood summers coming to me: drizzly beaches where my sister and I ate ice creams gritted with sand, or battered sausages and scraps out of newspaper, and Dad laughed while he wrestled with the striped windbreak. I remember my fascination with rockpools, sharp enough to cut your feet but full of treasures: hermit crabs poking alien legs from their faded, borrowed caves; pale pink Fibonacci sea-snails; tiny fish. Later, the arcades with their pinging buttons and garish colours. Time meant nothing at all to us. Our parents only argued on the way home in the car, never during the holiday, I think because they loved it as much as us, despite the cobwebby static caravan and the rainy days.

Sometimes I'll go up the road to Gold Stone, where the shingle gives way to soft sand and I can take off my shoes and watch the surfers at the mercy of the wind, kidding themselves for an hour or so that they are strong enough to control it.

Sunday 1st May 1988, 8.13 p.m.

I talked to Mum about those days on the beach we spent as kids. It's easier to talk about things in the distant past – they seem to have stayed with her.

"We couldn't afford to go abroad, and you know, people didn't really. There was rain, but always a couple of glorious days."

"I didn't want to go abroad," I told her. "I loved those trips."

She said she hated the static caravans and brought her own washing up liquid so she could spend the first afternoon scrubbing the sink. "Bloody filthy they always were." I suddenly remembered the crane flies that we called Daddy Long-Legs clinging to the corners of the caravan, leaving their fragile legs behind when we tried to brush them away with a rolled-up newspaper. Then I remembered my mother in her navy-blue swimsuit, legs curled under her on a beach towel, holding a book up to the sun.

"You look well today," Mum said. "You've put on weight; you needed to. You were skin and bones a few weeks back."

I told her I was trying to look after myself. Even now, though she doesn't always know me, her approval makes me glow.

When I came home on the bus, the sea mist of the morning had thickened to a dense fog that rolled right over the Headland. The foghorn blared out, deep like the call of some ancient kraken. My hair was soaked with damp five minutes after getting off the bus. I couldn't see Watchbell House in the mist and walked towards it unconsciously, letting my feet take the route they always take. It emerged like a shadow, a few shades darker than the fog itself, bright yellow windows marking it out as a house. Once inside,

I made coffee, wrapped my hair in a towel and sat with Wotsit for a while. I tried to watch a dating programme on TV, but it annoyed me, and the foghorn called out plaintively. I decided to work. I must be more disciplined and use the days where I can't be outside to paint inside, to return to what I used to love; paint through that feeling that I don't want to do it. I started with the mermaid's purse; here was an object some people have never seen. A silky but tough texture, smooth and dry with its four tendrils and its folded corners like a black envelope with its address written in black ink. As I mixed the colours, I realised there was a green quality to the black, so I combined Sepia, Hooker's Green and Ivory Black. But how to get that sense that, despite the tough casing, this contained nothing at all and was an empty casket? I realised then that watercolours wouldn't do; they are too delicate and mutable. I considered the squid ink I'd sometimes used at school. In minutes my skin smelt of brine and my fingers were stained with its brown-black hue, but the sketch I made was also too light and airy; the purse looked like it would give to the viewer's touch. Yet it isn't like this: it's hard, dried out and resistant. I would have to try oils, a medium I have not worked in in years. I set up my easel and went upstairs to find my oils, stored in a plastic box and still workable. When I was up there, I peered out of the window and could see nothing but vapour: fog covered Watchbell House. Even the bats had not flown – I heard them stirring in the eaves.

So, I have begun an oil painting which I'll work on every day. Oils need to be layered. The image needs to build. The paint takes years to dry out. But it's the only way to achieve the sense of solidity and emptiness, of an object being closed off and hollow inside, of the shadow of the thought that something once lived there.

Thursday 19th May 1988. Midnight.

I have worked on the oil painting every day since I last wrote. I kept the mermaid's purse on the windowsill and included the edge of the window in the work. I started on a day of fog and the fog crept into the following day, so the window has no landscape showing through its frame, just a thick texture of mist that can be seen through the pane. This means the purse becomes the sole focus of the painting, layers upon layers of different shades of black. I'm working larger than life size: a canvas about the size of my body, heavy and in the way whenever I want to reach the kitchen to make tea. The light changes, altering the shine and shadow on the object, giving it depth every time I return to the work. But today was supposed to be the day I finished the painting, the day the scent of earth and potatoes, oil and turpentine, those peculiar smells that an oil painting fills the room with, would be allowed to dry. The purse in the painting looked beautifully opaque, hard and resistant, the delicate tendrils curling at its corners, the flaked windowsill providing a contrasting texture, and the mist beyond the window suggesting the object would never give up its secrets. Today was a day of mist again after many days of clear weather, after vistas of racing clouds and purple-tipped waves, of sunlight rushing across the shingle and viper's bugloss battered in the wind. Today the window framed the fog again and the foghorn sang its lonely song to the boats lumbering in the sea. Today I returned from work to finish the painting, to add some tiny details of light and shadow and to sign my name. And I glimpsed, as I stared at the mermaid's purse, something beneath its surface, some shadow drifting and lit with a dark red light: a pulse of a being. It is not empty as I believed. Something grows inside the brittle skin.

Friday 3rd June 1988. Late.

Strange times. There is definitely something moving beneath the skin of the mermaid's purse: a dark, shifting shadow with limbs. It grows and as it grows, the purse grows with it. I cannot see its growth happening, and for days at a time the shadow itself disappears, but each morning I can tell the purse is bigger. It now sits fatly on the table like a cushion. Soon it will be the size of the representation in my oil painting: almost the size of me. I think of the rays or sharks that Solomon said grow in the mermaid's purse. I wonder if I should take it down to the sea. Instead I watch it and wait. Wotsit slinks around in the garden, which is abundant with pale dog roses, fennel, gorse and some strawberries I am trying out (these need so much water and are not taking well to the salty south-westerlies).

Seb came by unexpectedly yesterday evening. Solomon was not with him, and I have not told Solomon about it. There was a hard knock at the door.

"Hello, Dolly." Seb laughed and stepped in, the smell of beer on his breath. "More painting, I see. Well, this is a bit weird." He lolled over to the canvas.

"It's still wet," I said, as he put his fingers out to touch it.

"Oh, sorry." He leant up against the kitchen counter and folded his arms. "You know there were protestors again, at the plant?"

I said nothing; I hadn't known.

"Got in the bloody papers this time. They're sending in inspectors next month because years back there was a safety issue, worn-out equipment. And I suppose the pressure from the press…"

"Don't worry," I said. "It's probably a good thing; get an official bill of health. Then maybe they'll leave you alone."

"You don't get it," he said. He put his head in his hands. Then he looked up and sighed. "Do you know what radiation poisoning does to a person? Do you know, Dolores?"

"I can't say I've really thought about it…"

"A slow death. All your cells break down – it dismantles you at the smallest level… Unmakes you. It's not like death – it's dissolution."

My skin prickled. I thought of Violet shrinking away before my eyes; being fixed into a definite form was death for her. For us, it seems like the other way around. The mermaid's purse sat like a black hole on the table. Seb caught me looking at it.

"What is that bloody thing?"

"Solomon tells me it's a mermaid's purse, from the beach. An egg pouch."

"I know what a mermaid's purse is, Dolores, and that isn't one. It's huge. It smells bad too, like fish rot."

For a moment, I thought he'd take it and I was terrified again, but instead he pushed himself off the kitchen counter, and lurched to the front door, knocking the canvas to the ground as he did so. He looked at it but made no move to pick it up.

"You're a weirdo, Dolores Poole. I don't care what's bloody happened; you're not one of us with your art, the crap you collect, always here on your own…"

I inhaled sharply.

"You should live in town where you belong, not here in your holiday home playing at being a Headlander. And you should leave my brother alone; you're messing with his head."

He slammed the yellow door, and Wotsit sprang off the sofa to hide behind my legs.

The shape inside the mermaid's purse swam into sight, then fluttered like a fly caught against a windowpane.

Sunday 19th June 1988, 8 p.m.

I watch the purse each day. Dark shadows swimming beneath its surface. Impossible to add these to my painting now, where the image is fixed and opaque. It's been hot: cloudless skies; seakale smelling of honey, viper's bugloss, electric purple, growing everywhere on the shingle. Tourists have been posing against the sea mine, and the narrow-gauge train clatters by, children waving from the carriages. Every day after work I walk the beach until the sun goes down and stains the horizon Burnt Umber and Viridian. I drink tea and watch the bats flutter out at dusk, and I watch something beating like a heart beneath the skin of the mermaid's purse.

On Saturday I ran out of milk, so I went to Café Ferdinand for breakfast. I saw Solomon's fishing boat on the glittering horizon, saw him throw out a dark net. I traipsed up the shingle until it turned into dunes, long scrubby grass and the heat of the sun already at my back. Randy was wiping the counter; I saw her through the window moving to the sound of the radio. The bell chimed as I opened the door.

"Dolly, always a pleasure to see you."

"You too," I said. She set a steaming mug of coffee at my chosen window seat. "Sorry, Randy, can I have tea?" The smell of the coffee was too much. She frowned.

"You usually love this."

"I know, just for some reason…" (I know the reason; I just don't dare to believe it.)

She took it away and came back with my tea, some scrambled eggs and sausages, bacon, toast and a fried tomato, which I tucked into. She sat opposite me with a tea of her own. We were the only ones there, early on a Saturday before the hungover tourists started to rumble in, getting ready for their days of rock pooling and sunbathing, trips on the railway past the backyards of the residents, climbing up the old lighthouse.

"We don't get to talk often," Randy said, red lips at the rim of her cup. "How's life with you at the moment?" She's all but lost her Texan drawl, but I still detect it when she's really looking out for me.

"Okay," I told her. "A little strange; the other day…"

I found myself telling her about Seb's visit. "I know I can be a bit eccentric with the things I choose to paint, but there are other artists around here. And I know I wasn't born here…But he never used to have a problem."

Randy sat up a little straighter, propping her chin on her hands.

"Did he scare you, Dolly?"

I thought about it. Yes, he did; I felt threatened. But I didn't know what he was threatening me with. So, I said, "No, he didn't. I wouldn't use that word. It's silly to say, but I want the people who live here to like me."

Randy reached across and held onto the crook of my elbow where my arm rested on the table.

"They do. We all do," she said. "Let me tell you: Sebastian has not been okay since his granny Irene was killed in that storm. The storm itself did something to him. And the protestors at the plant, well that has unsettled him even more. He's become obsessed with what happened in Chernobyl. Morbid. Keeps clipping pictures of victims out of foreign papers. It's not about you." She paused and took a swig of her tea. "If you ask me, he should get out of that job. Thank goodness his brother has got his head screwed on. A local told me: as a kid Seb was always volatile. Solomon kept him out of trouble."

Randy sipped her tea again and glanced out of the window at the hot, breezy day. Some customers were making their way up the dunes towards us: a slim young woman with her dark hair pulled back, her boyfriend carrying a windbreak and a backpack, both laughing. I suppose Adrian and I used to be like this.

Randy turned back to me. "Seb should get out of that job. Perhaps even away from the Headland. They have lived here most of their lives. It's a beautiful place, my lovely, don't get me wrong. Texas is beautiful too, but it keeps you healthy up here –" she tapped her head – "if you see the world. If you meet people who are not like you. I know this well."

The bell jangled as the couple came in, and it was only then that I realised a little boy was following behind them, corn-coloured hair and freckled, wearing oversized swimming trunks and a T-shirt. Immediately, my impression of them shifted. They guided him to the table next to mine and lifted him onto a chair. His head only just reached the table top and he rested his chin there and gazed solemnly at me.

"We saw a kite," he said.

"Good weather for it," I replied, realising he was talking to me.

"It had a man at the end of it." His father smiled at me, half apology, half pride.

"Brilliant," I said.

"And what's that big spiky ball near the sea?"

"Oh, you mean the sea mine?"

"Is it yours?"

"No. A mine is actually a kind of bomb. But don't worry; it doesn't work anymore because it's so old."

"What is a bomb for?"

"Well…" I glanced at his mother, looking for help in this dangerous territory, but she was reading the menu. His father was lost in thought out of the window. They both looked tired now I could see their faces up close. "People used not to get along and to be mean to each other. To start wars."

"Grandpa was in the war," he said.

"Exactly. So that's where the sea mine came from. We don't need to hurt each other now, so…" I didn't like the lie of this, but I didn't want it to get complicated.

"Grandpa has a bit of bullet in his leg. He says it hurts when the air is damp."

"He's very brave."

"That is true…I'm going to have a sausage sandwich with brown sauce. My name's Max and I'm five and three months."

"Pleased to meet you, Max. I'm Dolores, Dolly for short."

He giggled, perhaps about my name. Then he said, "I can see a glow around you. Are you a superhero?"

I turned around to look behind me, thinking he must be seeing someone or something else, but when I turned back, he was staring into my eyes, smiling. "And you smell of lemons. Like lemonade."

I didn't have an answer. As I tried to respond, his mother sighed and shrugged.

"Leave this nice lady alone now," she said, pushing a strand of hair back behind her ears. She had evidently heard every word.

Back on the beach I felt tearful but couldn't explain to myself why. Perhaps I am spending too much time alone again. The little conversation had somehow cut into my heart like a wire; you wouldn't see the damage, but it was there: a clean slice. I wandered around the old, shipwrecked boats, some with their romantic names still visible: *Salty Pete; White Belinda; Diving Belle; Seas the Day; Sundown; The Flying Fish.* People sat on the porches and decks of their cottages, looking out at the shining sea. Back at Watchbell House the garden is thriving, if a little scorched around the edges. Inside, there was a smell of brine, vinegary and sexual, and the mermaid's purse was bigger than ever. It was glowing light red, like the glow of the thin skin of an ear caught in sunlight, and now a new feature: a hairline crack has opened along its centre, where that dark shape, if I watch for long enough, drifts and writhes.

And today, I went to see my mother. She was foggy again and didn't know me, her knitting falling from her needles, spilling her tea into her lap.

I don't want to write about her tonight.

I'm hoping for rain next week to ease the parched garden.

Tuesday 28th June 1988, 4 p.m.

Another hot day. There is a hosepipe ban, so I got the water-
ing can out and spent hours giving the garden a drink.
Deep green broom with its golden flowers growing over
the back window. Lots of wild mint, which I'm collecting
in a jar for my tea, since I have gone off coffee. A froth of
white elder and the last of the irises, which were looking
at me like they know me but can't quite remember from
where. Goldfinches bouncing around and fat, white-tailed
bumblebees going into the cups of every flower. Wotsit
is after the lizards again where they bask on the baking
stones. They are too quick for him, still as flint then off
as soon as he looks at them. The cornflowers are coming
up, electric blue and spiky. It's so hot the horizon fuzzes.
I see only the blurred outlines of people picking their way
along the shore. The seakale smells strong at this time of
year, of honey and musk. Seb told me once that it is good
at accumulating radiation from the power station, absorbing it like a sponge. I think about working on my triptych
again, but instead I set up my easel in the porch and make
a watercolour sketch of everything in the garden.

Out of the haze I see Solomon is coming towards me, sunburned and carrying two seabass, gulls wheeling above
him. No doubt he'll want to skin and gut the fish in my kitchen, roll them in flour and fry them in the skillet I haven't
washed. The mermaid's purse is hidden behind my painting of it. An evening with Sol after a hot day in the garden.
We'll sit outside with a beer and watch the sun drop down.

The last real conversation Morgan had with his mother was here at Watchbell House, at the little oak table, looking through its glass to the power station. Her hair had started to grow back, but she still wrapped a blue silk scarf around it. Her face was pale and thin. She held her mug with both hands. She barely ate the meal she'd made for them, whilst he finished his own, and then her leftovers.

"I love to see you eat," she laughed. "Silly, but I still think of you as a growing lad." She sighed into her mug and sipped. "Thanks for coming to the Headland – I know it's a trek from the city. I feel like you haven't been here in ages."

"I haven't," he said, "but I do like to come."

She looked at him then, her green eyes searching his face. She'd become watchful, like an animal, often saying nothing for long minutes, as if looking for something in his face. Morgan felt that the illness, or the drugs to treat it, were responsible for this dreamy state.

"Morgan," she reached to clasp his hand across the table; her grip was loose and weak. "I want to tell you something. And I want you to be…brave."

He felt like a child, fallen, with shingle embedded in his knees, being promised an ice cream to stop his tears.

"The treatment is not working. We…we thought that might happen. It's all come back. All over my body. And there isn't much point in giving me any more. So, that's it now." Her grip tightened. Morgan couldn't find his breath and choked down a sob. He was not being brave. "It won't be very long. And – oh dear, my sweet boy, I am sorry…"

She stood up, came over to his side of the table and draped herself across his shoulders, breathing into the back of his neck. He held onto the top of her arm, drew her down to him. It wasn't her fault, so why was she apologising? He wished then that he had never gone anywhere, never left the flat on Second Avenue that started to feel so small, or at least had come to the Headland every summer to sit amongst its bleak beauty with her. As if reading his thoughts, she said, "I'm so proud of you, teaching in the city, doing something important. I loved my teaching – it kept me going in difficult times. I wish I was still doing it. Listen…" She rose and returned to her chair, sipping coffee and briskly rubbing her eyes. "Let's not be sad. Let's enjoy the last few weeks. Let's talk to each other. I have had a brilliant life, and you're the very best of it."

He had thought then about asking her who his father was, but it didn't seem like the time; the question felt selfish. He left it until it was too late, and he was holding her fingers as they curled around his in the hospital, and her breaths grew further and further apart, and the final one was a long, tired sigh. He thought of the cancer all over her, inside, like stars in her cells. Collapsing stars.

He sat with her body for a while, looking around the small room, watching the nurse confirm no pulse, no life, feeling her cool hand rest lightly on his back. He wondered how they did it, people helping others through the last days of their lives, watching the loved ones bewildered on plastic chairs, giving them bags of belongings as they leave; things that will never be needed again: a necklace, a fountain pen, a wristwatch.

He phones Maggie and asks her about conception dates, gestation, about the baby forming inside her, pulsing in the red dark. "Why so interested?" she said. "Worried about the due date? It doesn't mean much to be honest, they come when they are ready."

But Morgan is thinking about himself, his own beginnings, and wondering why his mother has not yet mentioned him. For surely, he is already there, growing in the darkness of her body. He is already there in the past, listening to the sea, and to Solomon's voice, and to the rain on Watchbell's windows, and to the liquid shushing of the coastal breeze.

Thursday 7th July 1988. Early morning.

The most extraordinary thing has happened. Last night I returned from a day combing the beach and tending the garden (school is out for the summer now). I ate dinner and watched TV and drank mint tea outside. Then I went back in and read the newspaper on the sofa. I dozed a little with Wotsit needling at my feet, teasing with his claws. I woke drowsily to a cracking sound, like ice in a glass. I came to fully and looked around, the last traces of a dream whispering away. A scent of honey and iron wafted from the window – but the smell was so strong it must also have been in the house. A loud crack, and this time I twisted my neck (too afraid to move the rest of my body) to see the canvas was tipped to the floor and the mermaid's purse was bulging and writhing and had a deep fissure down its length.

Suddenly, it burst open. The scent of brine and burnt sugar. I got up slowly, crept towards it and knelt beside it. There were no lights on; I saw it only by the bright moon and the dim glow of the power station. There was a sac inside, pale red and twisting with a coiled shape. There I was, midwife at a dark birth, and like a good midwife I kept my distance. The sac burst and a black liquid poured out. It seeped into the cracks in the floorboards. Out of the liquid, something tumbled, leaving the broken pieces of the mermaid's purse behind. It flopped, slick, onto the floor, and its spindled limbs twitched. It was wet, very dark, folded in on itself.

Nothing happened for a long time after that. I examined it. Like Violet, it was hard to look at, but in a different way. It was so dark it was beyond the colour black, blacker than Carbon Black or Lamp Black. It seemed to swallow light, so that it was almost a negative, an absence of itself, a space where it should have been. The glimmer of wetness made it easier to see. My heart was hammering, and I tried to hold my breath. I glanced over at Wotsit, who slept soundly on the sofa. The burnt sugar smell faded, and it smelled only clean, like mint. My legs were cramped where I crouched on the floor. As it dried, I saw the surface of its folded body appeared like fur or feathers. I reached out to touch it and it felt more like the silky skin of a bat's wing, but its surface ruffled in the slight breeze from the open window. Despite the hot night, it was cool to the touch, but where I had placed just a fingertip, that spot grew warm as if it drew heat from me. It made no sound.

I had watched the mermaid's purse grow and seen this creature forming inside it, but somehow, I had not imagined this would happen. I had been in denial, ignoring its existence. I saw now that it pulsed with life, a heartbeat. The purse had been a kind of chrysalis after all, and this was some dark butterfly, a miraculous rearrangement of Violet's dead cells. I knew in my soul it was some version of her. It had to be. She had died and left me with the hand-sized mermaid's purse, cold and inert, and this huge living thing had grown from it. But this was also something else entirely. I understood it was both her and not her at the same time and accepted the contradiction.

I watched it for a long while as it slowly dried off in the hot night. At some point, hours and hours later, it was dry, its feathers black and bright as the galaxy above my roof, as the tarred boards of Watchbell House. With a sudden and weird motion, it awkwardly unfurled. I thought of those early flying machines of skin and wood as its "wings" cranked and rolled outwards. Their movement blew the hair back from my face. The wings were massive, touching the walls and the ceiling, and inside them was one big black space flashing with images in negative. Dark upon dark. Shadows on the night. I felt dizzy, as if I might fall in. I stared into the nothingness that is also a living creature. I feared it and where it could take me.

I desired it too.

"Welcome back," I whispered.

Friday 8th July 1988. Night.

I spent the day trying to work out what this new creature wants. Its dark furred wings absorb any source of light. Wotsit does not seem fazed; he approached it, sniffed it and passed it by. It is very still most of the time. It floated up and settled hugely into the corner of the ceiling, wings moving slightly in the breeze from the open window. I tried to offer it water and food (various fruits, even some of Wotsit's cat food), my paint box, some old newspapers. It did not respond to these. I looked up and stared into its centre, like night and moving with images. After a while I made out the impossible silhouettes on the even darker background. Watching them gave me a kind of vertigo or travel sickness, but I watched and watched until I deciphered what I think is a message. At first, a round, domed shape. Then something long and curved like a wall. Then a house which I recognised as the boarded shape of Watchbell. Then a spiked, round shape. Then a spiral, like a snail's shell. Then a triangular structure. It took a while for me to make out these images, and I grabbed my pad and sketched them in ink as they cycled across the creature. They were so different from the images Violet had created. They were colourless, they were ordered and logical. They did not come directly from experience in the moment but issued from the creature and they were repeated in the same pattern over and over.

After sketching them, I stood back to see the dark shapes on the white paper. I have worked out what they are. Sound mirrors first, both the round one and the long, rectangular one; Watchbell House; the sea mine; a shell (this one I was not so sure about); a fishing boat. I didn't know what any of it meant, but the images cycled through with such consistency and urgency, I knew it was a message. It was as if the previous Violet had learned, through practising making images of much of what she saw, how to create this one specific set of pictures. My first thought was that I needed to take her to these places, perhaps she wants to go to them. I remembered Violet at the sound mirrors, the powerful vibrations she made, the stones on the path lifting.

I fear taking this new creature anywhere but have decided I will do it weeknights at dusk. Dusk is late in the summer; the hazy light and her dark shadowy self will hopefully mean she cannot be seen, and by the time we return to Watchbell, it will be dark. Whether or not others can perceive this new version of Violet, I cannot tell. But what I feel is that she shouldn't be here. She needs to go to where she belongs and will be welcomed back, though I have no idea where that might be. But she knows. I must not fail her this time. I must help keep her safe, to get her to where she can live and thrive.

Sunday 10th July 1988, 11.15 p.m.

The bats shift and flutter in the roof; I can't see them, but I know they are there above me. I have become a night owl. School's out, so I can sleep late, like a teenager. In the night, I listen to the bats and watch Violet, now roosting too in a sense, wings folded, high up in the corner of my room, so dark she looks like a hole in the ceiling. The same images flash across her. I have taken her to these places at dusk as the Headland finally begins to cool each day. She travels above my head, soundlessly, the occasional beat of her huge wingspan ruffling my hair, her darkness keeping me in shadow. The sound mirrors, fringed with midges and capped with gulls, swallows spinning in the sky and swans cutting through the lake. Electric blue damsel flies hovering across the path. Finches settling in for the night and green moths waking up, heading towards the moon, catching themselves on Violet's wings.

The sea mine, inert and spiked with barnacles with a new fur of lichen, lapped by the grey-blue tide. I have taken her only to wrecked or resting fishing boats – I don't know if she wants one on the sea. All reek of herring and tumble with turquoise crab baskets, are littered with flashing scales and the remnants of claws and tiny bones. She hovers, she moves above it all, but nothing has happened. I cannot find a spiral shell, though I comb the beach every day.

It is Sunday and the first time I have not been to visit Mum. I feel terrible about it. But I want to protect this new version of Violet; I can't let anything happen this time. It is a second chance. What if I left her, even for the afternoon, and when I returned, she was gone? But I also wonder: am I making an excuse to avoid my mother, who is showing signs of decline? She has good days where she knows me and is the woman I know. Days when she takes my face in her hands and kisses me like a child; when she looks up shrewdly from her teacup and tells me some difficult truth. But then she has bad days when she's knitting some shapeless thing because she's forgotten whether it's scarf or a glove, or she peers at me as if through a blizzard, or worse, she is afraid of me and calls the staff to arrest the intruder. Days when she asks me to tell my sister to put out the rubbish, or my dad to drive me to netball practice. Or when she weeps because she knows something is very wrong with her but cannot put her finger on what.

So, today I telephoned her instead.

"Cassie?" she said.

"No, it's Dolores. Dolly."

"Put your sister on, love, I need to speak to her."

"She's not here, she's in Seattle, remember?"

"So where are you, Dolly-mixture?"

"The Headland."

"Come out of your head, my love; it's not a good place to stay for too long,"

"No, the Headland, where the holiday home is. It's summer so…"

"You and Adrian by the sea? He's not making you do all the cooking, is he? You deserve a break. And he needs to forget the city for a bit. Do him good."

"He's not…It's just me here today."

"You love the sea. Do me a painting of it. You are so good at painting…"

I suddenly remembered the long reams of printer paper my dad used to bring back from work, striped and green at the back, tantalizingly white on the other side, long enough for whole drawn or painted panoramas that stretched over the entire living room floor. I remembered a snail I'd watched climb the wall of our house for weeks, only to see it shattered into a thousand pieces on the patio, two-dimensional as a jigsaw. My finger slammed in the back door by the wind as I ran to see my dad return from work. A splinter from the garden fence in my palm when I was learning to roller-skate. A drawing pin I stood on that went through my red towelling sock and into my heel. The memories tumbled into my head as if someone had knocked them off a high shelf. My mother was there, every time, her arms around me.

"I love you," I said to her. The phone crackled for a moment.

"I love you too, Dolly-mixture mine. Never forget that."

Friday 29th July 1988. Late morning.

The garden thrives. Crickets everywhere, clacking amongst the poppies. And the poppies, deep red and pink and orange. Butterflies: painted ladies, peacocks and cabbage whites among the lavender. Bees too, the whole place thick with their fuzzy vibrations. Yellow St. John's wort and ripe blackberries. There was a fine mist of rain yesterday, but this has burnt away, leaving only a dry breeze and low, heavy clouds hanging fatly in the sky.

I take this version of Violet out every dusk and visit the places that flash across her form. The last time we went to the sound mirrors, she hovered above me and seemed about to ascend, but then turned and moved silently back along the gravelled path of the nature reserve. Fat yellow-and-black caterpillars hung in the hedges. She went ahead of me for a moment and swooped close to the ground. The moon was coming up and the sun had left a gash of Raw Umber at the horizon. The moon floated lime-green above the lake. Violet does not usually get so close to the ground, but she had folded herself over something on the path. As I caught up, I saw it was a dead rabbit, delicate fur lifting in the evening breeze, a bloody strip of it torn away, glassy eyes half eaten by maggots. I guessed it had been there a few days at least. Perhaps it had myxomatosis or had just lost its way and succumbed to the heat or was killed by some great bird and then abandoned. Violet was feeding from it somehow, enveloping it with her wings. She made a sound like someone inhaling very deeply, the only noise I have heard from her in this new incarnation. I watched, mesmerized. Once she had finished, she drew away with one smooth beat of her wings and hovered above me again like a cloud. The rabbit on the path had turned from brown to grey, as if it had become a black-and-white photo of its previous self.

We also venture along the beach, passing by the power station and the cliff-dwelling birds happy to use it as a substitute. The other night, the tide was low, exposing oozing mud and bleached animal skulls and leaving dozens of jellyfish stranded, collapsed balloons of bioluminescence reflecting the stars, never going back where they belong. Violet wrapped herself over these too and inhaled their last flickers of life.

<u>Monday 1st August 1988, 11.45 p.m.</u>

It's my birthday today. This isn't where I imagined I would be in my life. I pictured myself with Adrian. With you. But I made myself breakfast, put some late roses from the garden in a vase. Drank a pot of tea. I took out your box and opened it, looked at your few things. Turned them over in my hands, touched what I have left. Pitiful really. Pointless. I put the lid back on and tied the ribbon tight, replaced the box on the top shelf in the oak cupboard upstairs. Violet breathed like a velvet bellows on the ceiling and the images cycled darkly at her heart. If only this was language, but it isn't quite that. No more than a painting is language. It doesn't speak directly. It has no grammar, but it must be interpreted. Violet the artist.

In the evening I agreed to meet Sol at the Hope and Anchor. It was a humid night and the stars looked smudged and out of focus. Sol was with Seb on the veranda, and as I approached from the beach below, I could tell they were arguing. They didn't see me in the dusk, and I hesitated beneath them.

"It's not right," hissed Seb. "There is something not right about her, about that house. She's hiding something." I saw his shadow shift where he leaned over the balustrade. Froth from his pint dripped down his arm as he gesticulated. Then came Solomon's voice, deep and calm.

"Don't be daft, Seb. What could she be hiding?"

"There were high readings in her house."

"But they took that away. Contaminated driftwood, wasn't it? It happens, you know that."

There was a pause, both men gulping from their glasses.

"I'm a little worried about you, Seb. All those pictures you've got of the Chernobyl thing."

"It's not me," Seb told him, a sigh in his voice. "It's the protestors around the plant all the time. They told me to look it up, to read for myself. They have a point."

"Still, you need not get obsessed with it."

"I don't like her, Sol. She's not a Headlander. She's not supposed to be here permanently. It's a holiday house. Her paintings are so fucked up. They didn't used to be. It's like she's stuck here, after what happened. She needs to just go back where she belongs."

I held my breath.

"And you. I know you like her, Sol, but I think she's messing you around."

They talked on, Sol trying to defend me, Seb suspicious. I heard something important though: Sol telling Seb he loved him, he was his brother and that was that. His voice was tender. "Little brother," he said, "I hate to see you like this. I'll make it right. You'll be okay." And I knew from the way Sol said it that Seb was the most important thing and was always going to be. Only Claire came as close.

I walked quietly around to the front of the pub, ordered a gin and tonic and stepped out onto the veranda. I glanced up at the moon, hanging there as if hastily sketched. The Milky Way dusted a sky not yet dark. Prussian Blue, with a hint of Hooker's Green, a drop of Indigo. I smiled and they turned to me, as if coming out of a dream, as if suddenly remembering who I was.

"Happy birthday," they said together, and raised their glasses.

When Seb went to the loo later, Sol reached over and hooked my fingers into his own.

"I hope you're okay," he said. "I hope it's an okay kind of birthday."

I smiled and sipped my drink. He told me how worried he was about Seb, glancing back towards the bar to see if he was coming. "He's always been a bit more anxious than me, prone to letting his imagination get the better of him. But since the storm…" He sighed and looked down into his empty glass. "He needs to leave the plant. Being there is no good for him. He's imagining all sorts of terrible things. He even has a recurring nightmare, where the whole thing explodes and there is nothing left of the Headland."

"Those are just dreams," I told him, "I'm sure everyone has them in these uncertain times. But you're right that he should leave; living inside a bad dream is no good."

Seb came out then from the brightness of the pub. He smiled thinly at me and raked his hand through that grass-straight hair. "Another round?" Sol said yes, but I told them I was tired and fine to walk home alone. Sol didn't like this, but said he'd watch me as I went back up the beach.

I'm content now, here on the sofa, stroking the thin skin of Wotsit's ears. Violet is spread out above me on the ceiling.

Violet is the night sky.

She is a great, mythical bear.

She is the black water on the lake.

The shadows of the sound mirrors.

Violet is a murmuration of starlings.

A murder of crows.

Violet is an ancient cave.

The blood streaming in my veins.

A hieroglyph.

She is deep sea.

Violet is the static on the TV screen.

She is the pupil of my eye.

She is a leaf falling.

She is the rubbed-out end of the rainbow.

Violet is a chrysalis.

She is roadkill.

She is the first catch.

A total eclipse.

Violet is the eye of the storm.

Thursday 4th August 1988. Early.

Something terrible happened.

We came home from a walk, Violet and I. It was still warm, but blustery and near dusk when we returned. Wotsit was in the garden, lying very still on his side near the decorative flints. At first, I thought he was sunning himself, catching the last oblong of warmth on the stones. But as we drew closer, Violet hovering above me, I saw he was trembling, his tongue sticking through his teeth, a trail of vomit coming from his mouth. The thin skin of his third eyelids was visible and his eyes were rolled back into his skull. I was so afraid of the death I saw coming for him, I had to brace myself to touch him and carry him, already stiffening, into the house.

Violet made a low humming sound like a refrigerator. She spread herself over the ceiling, a black, feathery canopy, whilst I lay Wotsit on the sofa. I called the vet. He couldn't come straight away because of another emergency. He suspected rat poison, and that there might be little he could do. He told me to sit tight, try water and keep Wotsit warm. Comfort is what he really meant. Hold him while he dies. Make him believe it is nothing to be afraid of. The water came back out between the sharp little teeth. I couldn't bear to watch him shivering.

Then I felt a pain in my own head, so sharp I lost balance and crouched down on the floor. Violet peeled herself from the ceiling, humming like a power saw and hot as an oven. She enveloped Wotsit's little body, and I thought with horror that she was consuming him. There was a sucking sound, a gurgling and a panicked bleat that might have come from Wotsit or Violet, or both of them. Violet's winged body writhed. I tried to scream "Stop!" but this came out as a whisper and I couldn't stand up. The floorboards and the windowpanes hummed. My ears fizzed.

Then it stopped. Violet folded up like an umbrella and shot up the staircase into the bedroom. My head cleared.

Wotsit was still on the sofa, but bright and awake, grooming himself.

When the vet came to the house, he was angry with me. "Nothing wrong with him, Ms. Poole. I think, if you don't mind me saying, it's you that needs some rest."

The following morning, I saw Seb and Solomon at Café Ferdinand and I told them about it.

"He was very ill, but he recovered thankfully. I did think…I did think for a moment that he would die. It was poison, I'm sure of it. But I can't understand where it came from."

Seb told me they use poison near the plant sometimes, behind the work cafeteria, but never beyond its gates.

"Seems insane," said Solomon. "All the protected wildlife around here. Surely they can't."

"I don't know," countered Seb, staring at his brother over his cup. "Seems people do whatever they want to do sometimes, no matter the consequence."

"But," I said, "Wotsit never goes as far as the plant."

"Well, perhaps, Dolly, but how do you really know? He is a cat after all."

And I suppose I don't know. I spent the afternoon hosing Watchbell's garden with water, never mind the ban. The poison must be invisible. I hope it has washed away.

Sunday 7th August 1988. Late.

Season of illness, as if the heat is helping it to breed. Now my mother is not well, so I had to leave Violet today, tucked high in the ceiling of my bedroom, wrapped in her wings. When I got to the nursing home, Mum was in bed, striped blue bedspread pulled up to her chin. She looked like a little finch. A chest infection, the nurse said, and they had called in the doctor, who said she did not need to go to hospital and was better to stay in her home. I feel desolately guilty about not visiting her, as if that were the direct cause of her illness. The nurse was a big man with hairy arms, and he shuffled about pouring water into a cup and giving Mum her pills. She grinned at me just like she used to, and I realised that despite her illness, today she knew exactly who I was. I sat with her and stroked the white curls from her forehead. Her skin was as dry as old leaves. Her breath rattled in her throat. She didn't talk today. I talked instead, telling her about my garden, my walks to the nature reserve and along the beach. I listed everything that is growing. "I'm becoming quite the gardener," I said, "even in a dry, inhospitable garden." I thought of our childhood garden with its lush, mowed lawn and curved beds, an oak tree holding up a handmade swing.

"I go everywhere with a friend," I told her. "Violet. She's… she's keeping me company whenever Adrian's not around." At this she squeezed my hand, as if somehow, for a moment, she understood that Adrian had left me. As I spoke, her eyelids fluttered down and she drifted into sleep, her hands folded over her chest. My own chest felt heavy as I crept out of the room.

The bus back along the coast was acrid and hot, the windows levered open to let in only more hot air. Beach huts glowed along the shoreline of Gold Stone, as if about to burst into flames. I felt nauseous and got off a stop early, near Café Ferdinand, and decided to go in for a cold drink. Randy was there at the counter, talking to Solomon, who leaned down over a bottle of beer that he was peeling the label from. He looked clean out of the shower, dark curls still damp. As I got closer, I caught his scent of soap and salt. He gave me a half smile and squeezed my arm but looked grave. Randy did too.

"What's wrong?" I asked. He sighed and his eyes flicked back to Randy.

"Seb," he said.

My face flushed; I thought for a moment Randy had told him about my run-in with his brother and I had not wanted to upset him. Sol shifted on his stool, turning to face me,

"Protestors at the plant again on Friday. Then Seb sees one of them at the Ship Inn afterwards where he'd gone for a pint. Picks a fight with him for some reason – he's been friendly with them until now. It's like he just snapped. Beats him up pretty badly. The guy will probably press charges against Seb, and that's even more for the papers."

I said nothing for a moment, thinking of the conversation I'd overheard. Then, "What will you do?"

Randy looked between the two of us, drying mugs and hooking them above the counter. She poured me a glass of lemonade without asking what I wanted. I looked at the bead of moisture rolling down the outside of the glass; it was exactly what I wanted to take the edge off the bile rising in my throat. I felt a vibration in my belly, the weird pressure of a limb or skull. A thought of you flashed into my mind. I tried to ignore it. Sol took a sip of his beer, the bottle now blank.

"He'll have to leave the Headland. He certainly can't work at the plant anymore. But I think it's best he gets away. He hasn't been right since the storm."

Sol didn't want to talk much after that. He swigged down the last of his beer, and by way of a goodbye, touched his palm to my back. Randy raised her eyebrows as the bell tinkled above the closing door.

"It's for the best," she said. "Before Seb does anything really silly."

"I've got to go too," I said, pushing some coins across the counter. Randy pushed them back. I left my half-drunk lemonade, thinking of Violet, wanting to get back to my silent, shadowy friend.

There is a tap at the door, soft but unmistakable. Morgan is asleep on the sofa, the journal on the floor, sweat sticking his shirt to his back. One tap; he hasn't imagined it. Through Watchbell's yellow window he can see a man's profile; somebody waiting under the porch. He opens the door. It's the father from the beach, his previously anguished face impassive. He's alone and holds Morgan's cardigan, the one Morgan last saw draped over the shoulders of his eldest son. The dark wool smells of washing powder.

"Hello. I hope I am not intruding." The man hangs back on the doorstep. His eyes are shining and brown, his white shirt pressed and open at the collar. He wears black leather shoes that are old, but polished. The kitchen is messy, scattered with coffee grounds and crumbs, and there is a blanket screwed up on the sofa. Morgan whips it away. "Come in," he says, rubbing the back of his head. "I'm Morgan."

"Ervin." The man shakes his hand and steps softly over the threshold.

"Can I get you some coffee?"

"Water is fine. It is so hot today." He doesn't look hot, but cool and clean. He stands with the cardigan draped over his forearm and looks towards the fireplace, as if trying not to look around the room. His gaze lands on the painting and a slight frown troubles his face.

"Please, sit down. Sorry it's a bit messy. I wasn't expecting…"

"No, no. It's a lovely home." Ervin sits and Morgan lifts the cardigan from his arms.

"Thank you. I mean, your son could have kept this. I wouldn't mind."

"It is yours. I wanted to return it." Ervin sips his water. "And I wanted to thank you."

"Ah, well, I'm not sure I did anything…"

"You were there." Ervin holds the glass down and looks at Morgan. "You did not turn away."

There is a pause where Morgan also looks at the painting, the dark of the mermaid's purse shining.

"How are both your sons doing?"

Ervin's face relaxes, his expression shifts. For a moment, Morgan thinks he will cry. But a broad grin stretches across his face. "They are both fine. Shayan, my little one, is recovering but he's going to be fine. The fisherman saved him. I'm forever grateful, and forever in grief for that man. I will think of him every day."

Morgan looks at Ervin, wondering what desperate circumstances led his family to the violence of the sea.

"What will you do now?"

"There is a centre where we will stay until the paperwork is completed. Until we can find somewhere. It isn't like a home. But we are safe there and we will have food. Then I'll try to find work."

"What kind of work?"

"Anything, of course. My profession, back in Iran: I was a history teacher. But I doubt I will do that again. At the moment I cannot work. And I am only here visiting you as a special dispensation." He looks out of the window, and Morgan notices a figure facing away from them on the shingle, looking out to sea. He realises Ervin is not free. He has left a life so difficult he is willing to lose his freedom.

"I'm a history teacher too," says Morgan, surprised by the symmetry. "I'm so sorry about what you have been through."

Ervin rises and shakes Morgan's hand again, more firmly than the first time. "You're a good man, Morgan. A good man in a world where not everything is good. History doesn't always remember us."

Morgan does not feel good. He claps Ervin on the shoulder but cannot say anything.

Before long, he's watching him walk back along the shingle with his chaperone, his shoulders thin beneath the white cotton of his shirt, the sun bright on the calm water at the shoreline.

Thursday 11th August 1988. Late.

We Headlanders knew about the oil spill before it was reported in the local news; the normally clean salt shore was darkly rainbowed and the shingle had a slick gleam. Solomon brought dead fish and dead crabs back in his nets, and lined them up along the beach, black as their own shadows. He knelt before them and ran his hands along his unshaven cheeks. Late summer is beautiful, the clouds like peach skin, the hydrangeas in my garden turning green and papery. But at the edge of everything, the sea was poisoned. The tanker is called the *Prospero* and it collided with rocks, trying to avoid a fishing boat in the Channel. It bled and bled from its damaged hull. It wasn't an international disaster as it isn't a vast tanker, but it was a disaster for us.

I spent today with the Headlanders trying to clean sea birds. I felt sick touching them as they tried to move, tarred monsters, drowning in sludge. Solomon told me that crude oil is drilled out of the earth, that it is made from ancient dead creatures, zooplankton, algae, decomposed over millions of years into something else entirely, into dark energy. These dead souls, powering our lives. I thought of the holes piercing their resting places, underwater and deep in the rock. What should have remained buried and in the past, released in a rush of ink-black liquid.

I made myself touch the birds, washing their feathers in water and a special soap. I held them, covered in rot and breathlessness. I rinsed their fused beaks and their blinded eyes. We all did.

It struck me that grief is like this: a slick coating of death upon the living so that they cannot breathe, so that they are sticky with it, unable to stay above the waves. It struck me that I am like those birds.

In the night, everyone took a break and went to Café Ferdinand, where Randy opened up in the early hours to feed them all. And I took Violet out; she was restless, cranking her wings up and down. The sky was very dark and clear. She stretched her massive, creaky wings and beat them until she was out at sea, like a storm cloud on the horizon. My head started to throb, my abdomen tingled and my legs shook. The flat land vibrated, and the water churned. The world blurred for a moment and I passed out.

When I came to, I was in the garden of Watchbell House, my cheek against the sharp stones, and the sun was rising. I went into the house. It stank of decay, like the fish guts in the hull of Solomon's boat when he's cleaning it. Violet was stretched over the floor, pulsing. The images at her dark centre flashed as always, but there were others there, rippling across at intervals: pictures of tiny, simple-celled creatures. Zooplankton. Algae. I knew she had absorbed the oil from the sea. Millions of years' worth of dead creatures that used to creep and swim the earth and ocean. Before us and for aeons longer than us. All of their tiny deaths, their ancient time, she had drunk it in. The stench began to fade until it was just like damp soil, a hint of mollusc.

I knew, when I went back to the shore, there would be no more oil in the water. I opened my yellow front door and looked out. A crowd gathered, exhausted from the night before, staring amazed at the clean waves rushing backwards and forwards.

I don't know what this act has done to Violet, how it might have damaged her, or whether she thrives on this now. I wonder if it isn't death she has absorbed, but time, reeling it back, siphoning it away. I'm thinking now about how we run our own lives on these long-gone layers of other lives, so old we can barely conceptualise them ever having lived.

Saturday 20th August 1988. Afternoon.

In the days that followed the oil spill, I didn't take Violet out. What had happened was inexplicable, and I worried that people might become suspicious and find her. Experts combed the beach and took water samples from the shore. Where there had been a scum of emollient, creamy as mayonnaise against the dark rocks, there is now clear water. They found only slight traces of oil on the seakale and were not able to save all of the wildlife already affected, but the damage was slight compared to what they had anticipated. This was not the first oil spill. And I expect it won't be the last.

On Friday Solomon came grinning up the beach with a turquoise basket of living crabs. They were snapping and shining, the colour of Burnt Umber.

"The sea knows how to heal itself, given the chance," he declared. "There are lots of tiny creatures, too small to see, that can clean the water. And the power of the tides dissipating the oil." He lifted the clicking basket like a treasure chest. "Seems a shame to eat these crabs."

We ate them, nonetheless.

The Headlanders are out even more than usual, walking the hot, blustery shore, appreciating their home after seeing it almost ruined.

Violet breathes inside Watchbell House, breathes inside its tarred, black boards. Her body is like a shadow, pulsing in my time, but perhaps not wholly in my time, perhaps cycling through the sediment of other times, consuming them to keep my world clean, to keep me in the present.

Sunday 21st August 1988, 3.15 p.m.

A perfect day. Banks of creamy cloud, a salt breeze and not a soul on my part of the beach. I painted all day. I painted the mirage of France out beyond the horizon, allowing the watercolours to bleed and drip. Violet came to the porch of Watchbell House and formed a canopy above me, shielding my eyes from the sun. She seemed merely a soft membrane, a skin rather than a being. Light rebounded from the shingle and Wotsit slinked around the strawberry plants and elder bushes, hunting lizards. They outwitted him, still as rocks in the sunlight.

My brushes clinked in their shining jar of water. This may be what it feels like to belong somewhere. To know the sea accepts you at this shore and wants to shush you to sleep. To know someone is trying to understand you as I try to understand Violet. I watch her very skin, the messages imprinted on her body, in an effort to know her. And yet, even if I can't decipher them, it doesn't matter. It matters only that I try.

I know Violet does not belong here. I know I cannot make her stay. But for now, I am inside her shadow. I will stay for as long as I am able. For now, I am close to feeling peace.

Tuesday 23rd August 1988. Early hours.

Tonight, we went out again. Our walk took us past the sea mine, along the coast, where a few people still wandered (we hung back and nobody seemed to notice us) and, later than usual, along the gravelled path to the sound mirrors. The entrance to the edge of the lake is at the end of a street lined with bungalows and their immaculate lawns. I only turn on my torch after we have gone through the gate and are hidden by the thickets that line the path. This is not somewhere you would normally want to go at night. The lake shone intermittently, but dark clouds gathered over the moon and the dead stars emanating their historic light. It was humid, even so late, and sweat stuck my shirt to my skin. Night creatures scuttled ahead of us at the bends in the path, their eyes flashing in the torch beam, moths batting in the brambles, crickets rubbing their limbs together.

Violet swooped above me like a canopy, like my shadow if I were hanging upside down.

When we reached the sound mirrors, beyond the locked swing bridge on the other side of the water, she rose up and up, far from me, passing over to that strange island of concrete structures. She landed on top of the circular one, fifty feet high, sending a scatter of dozing birds away into the lowering clouds. My head ached, right into my cheeks, and I guessed a storm might come soon to relieve the long weeks of heat. She spread out her huge wings and there she was on the great stone ear, taking up half the sky.

I felt a vibration begin in my abdomen; it spread into my blood, down to my feet, through my fingertips. The lake wobbled and birds rose from it, shedding droplets of water into the air. The low hum intensified. I felt it in my eyeballs. The gravel on the path lifted and hovered. The clouds stopped moving and flexed. The sound was so low and loud I felt I would pass out. I wondered if it could be heard elsewhere. I grabbed the railing of the bridge and knelt on the ground, shaking. Violet was outstretched, the thin velvety texture of her wings vibrating. The sky around the sound mirrors flashed and rippled like shattered water. Out of her dark centre came a high, piercing note, a wail of anguish and fury and longing. Then I closed my eyes. Tears burned behind them, but I didn't cry, I slipped out of consciousness, my head shot through with pain. I curled up on the ground and longed for silence.

When I woke, I was wet with rain. I saw clouds in the distance, full and heavy, and heard thunder. A shard of lightning far off, near the old lighthouse, brightened the sky for a moment, and on the horizon, far away from me, was Violet, heading out to sea. I glimpsed her flight, only for a few seconds, her massive wings lazily beating. Then I was in darkness again on the wet ground. I fumbled for my torch but couldn't find it so traipsed blindly back along the path, catching my shirt on the brambles, seeing by the houses at the edge of the nature reserve that still had their lights on. By the time I reached the beach, the rain was hammering down, the thunder blasting out every minute. A great fork of lightning touched down into the sea, but I did not glimpse Violet again. I struggled with the door of Watchbell House and stumbled in, wet to the skin. The whole sky lit up and I saw the power station through the window, but no Violet, no Violet. Had she gone now, finally left me? Who was she calling to so furiously? Was someone coming for her to take her home? The heat of the last few weeks had released the storm which poured itself into a choppy black sea and over the parched seakale. I dried myself off and sat in my dressing gown staring out of the streaming window. What had my life become; wandering out at night with a strange being above my head, hiding most of the time from people that care about me, learning how to see what nobody else can see? What would I do now? How would I live?

My thoughts were interrupted by a flash of light from the power station – not lightning this time but issuing from the roof of the plant itself – then a distant rumble: an explosion. I looked through the streaming window to see a flurry of birds take off from the top of the station and wheel away. An alarm wailed, high enough to cut through the sound of the rain. I ran upstairs and put on clothes, then rummaged through the drawers; I had an evacuation card, we all did, issued in case the plant exploded. This occasion counted, though the plant was intact; something had blown. I rifled through the contents of the cutlery drawer but found nothing, lurching over, trying to pull my wellingtons on at the same time.

Where was I supposed to go? I couldn't remember.

Then: three loud knocks on the door.

"Dolores!" shouted Solomon from the other side. I opened it. There he was in a blue sou'wester, with a bag slung over his shoulder. "We need to get out of here." He strode into the living room and scooped Wotsit off the sofa, grabbed my hand and led us out into the storm.

Wednesday 24th August 1988. Midnight.

The contingency plan was to head to the Community Centre, with its low, corrugated roof and blank expanse of old wooden gym flooring. It didn't seem far enough away to me. We gathered there, some in pyjamas, some with bags, one person (the writer, I think, who stays in one of the cottages very near the power station every summer) without shoes on. Her toenails were painted bright red and her feet were sandy and nicked with cuts. The rain battered against the roof. Tony, the vicar, and his wife gave out tea. Seb paced at the end of the hall, avoiding everyone. Solomon talked to him for a while, but I watched Seb sling Sol's hand off his shoulder, and Sol walked back over after that. Gym mats and chairs were set out. Older people were offered chairs. I was offered a chair too. "I'm alright," I said. I could sit on a gym mat like everyone else. I stood most of the time anyway, looking at the felt board that advertised a Ford Orion for sale, Tupperware parties and an aerobics class. Wotsit sat with the writer on her mat whilst she stroked him, her eyes glazed, obviously elsewhere in her head.

"Something similar happened a few years ago," said Tony, who looked at me today and smiled. "Some faulty valve. There was a complete investigation afterwards." He seemed to be enjoying the occasion.

"You can't be too careful," said his wife, whose name I've never learned because Tony only ever introduced her with a flourish of his chubby hand as "My wife".

As it happened, we were given the all-clear three hours later, just before the biscuits ran out. Some people didn't leave right away, enjoying the too-strong tea and a chance to catch up. A rumour went around, mostly from Tony himself as he poured the tea, that the protestors had staged the explosion, to scare people, that it was on the outside of the building. A very risky thing to do, nonetheless.

"It's nice to see you looking so well," said the vicar's wife, appraising me as I wrapped my cardigan over my shoulders and picked up Wotsit. The rain had cleared, the humidity had eased, and there was finally a chill in the night air. "Thanks," I said, deciding I had known her too long to ask her actual name. I wonder if she remembers it herself.

I did not feel well, despite the night's freshness. I was slightly sea-sick, wobbling off my centre of gravity, overtired from my midnight walks and confused about Violet. Solomon took me to the door of Watchbell House. He said he wouldn't stay; he wanted to make sure Seb got home and calmed down. He would be waiting outside the Community Centre. Tony had strict instructions to keep him there until Sol got back. Seb had spoken to no one all night, and everyone avoided him too as they'd heard about the fight in the pub. But he'd caught my eye at one point and held it for a long time. Perhaps he had expected me to look away.

Sol took both my hands in his own (calloused but also worn smooth in places like beach glass). The air was light and seaweedy, and the calmed waves pushed the shingle softly over and over itself. Sol's eyes were black as tar in the clear night, so many stars behind him. He kissed the tips of my fingers and said, "Goodnight, Dolores; I'll see you again soon." He passed a sleepy Wotsit to me, then paced away through the garden and disappeared into the night.

I climbed the stairs to my room and undressed in the dark. It was only when I got into bed and put my head on the pillow that I saw her: Violet up in the ceiling, wings enveloped over the darkness at her centre so I could not see her cycling images. She was as silent as the grave.

Saturday 10th September 1988. Late.

Sol came by this evening. I suppose we have an unspoken agreement that on Saturdays we have dinner. I met him at the door, making sure Violet was in my bedroom. Sol cooked crab and put it into some fresh bread. I said we should sit outside; it was still mild even though the nights are drawing closer. He was very quiet today after dinner. We sipped beer and watched people walking their dogs in the distance. The underbellies of the clouds turned pink with a stain of grey. I couldn't think of the proper names for the colours. I asked about Seb. Sol narrowed his eyes.

"He's accepted he's got to leave. But he doesn't want to. I'm not sure how he'll fare. I'm sorting out a job for him in the city – you know, we have family there."

"Maybe when things calm down again, he can come back?"

"Maybe." Sol sighed and looked away from me towards the sea.

"I won't stay," he said after helping me wash up the plates. He rolled his sleeves back down and buttoned them methodically as he talked. I felt I'd perhaps done something wrong, that I was in some way to blame for everything and that he was angry. You never know with Solomon. I hugged him and he set off back to his cottage. It was dark by then and I didn't see him out. I went straight to my room with a mint tea. Evenings are chillier now, but I welcomed that.

I sat on the bed and watched Violet. She was up in the corner of the ceiling, her wings outstretched and flexing, showing me her cycle of images. Watchbell house…the sea mine…the spiral shape…the fishing boat. I realised the sound mirrors were now missing from the sequence. Had she already done what she needed to do there? I made a mental note to take her to the sea mine on our next evening walk; that was now first on her list.

Then Sol was at the door of my room.

"Dolores, Dol," he said softly, pushing the door right open and sitting tentatively on the bed next to me. I held my breath and glanced up to the ceiling, but his gaze didn't follow mine. He stared at my face and took my hands between his dry, rough palms.

"I'm sorry I just left," he said, his voice low, "I wanted to tell you something. I know you haven't asked me to do anything with our current…situation. But I wanted to tell you I might have to leave, with Seb, at least for a little while until he gets on his feet." He paused and watched my face. I couldn't speak. "I can't leave him alone," he continued, "but…" and then a long exhalation, a breath like a gust from the sea that he'd been holding in his lungs for months, "I love you, Dolores Poole, and I don't want to leave you."

"I…" I started to tell him. All of the things I thought I couldn't say and wouldn't acknowledge now crowded at my lips. Then Sol glanced up. His eyes scanned the ceiling. A day's growth of stubble at his neck – I counted the little black dots. He frowned, dark brows knotting. His hold on my hands loosened and he half stood up. Violet's wings were still unfurled, huge and quivering, and her dark heart still played a loop of its even darker pictures.

Sol's hand went up to his mouth. He saw her, clearly, as I do.

"What the bloody hell is that?" His voice came out in a low whisper.

"Listen," I said, still sitting in bed. "It's okay; she won't hurt you."

"She? What the fuck, Dolly?" He tugged my arm, trying to get me to stand. Then he looked down at me in horror.

"We've got to…"

"No, Sol, she's not dangerous." He let go of me and backed into the doorway.

"Some kind of fucking mutated bat," he muttered, mainly to himself. "How long has it been there?"

"She hasn't always been like this," I said. I stood up. I had never tried to explain to anyone else, and now I finally could, there didn't seem to be a way of making sense of it. There wasn't any language.

"I've got to think," Sol muttered.

"She…she grew. She was smaller, then she died. And you know. The mermaid's purse," I said – Sol would understand this – "the one I was painting?" Sol stared at me and ran his hand slowly down the length of his face. "Yes," he said. I knew he would get it.

"After she died, she grew again in there, in the mermaid's purse. And she…sort of hatched. And now she's like this. I think she only wants to go home. She needs my help."

"And what was it – she – like before?"

"Before, she was lighter, brighter. But hard to see, almost impossible. She would…change every second. She was here once, when you came, right in front of your eyes. And it was her who absorbed the oil spill, why it wasn't as bad as they said."

Sol paused; his posture softened, and he said, "Will you come downstairs, Dolly? Tell me all about it down there?"

He was listening. He was going to help me. I was so relieved to be able, finally, to share this with someone else. Of course: Solomon, I knew he would understand. I knew he would be able to see her. He guided me gently out of the room and took one more look at Violet before clicking the door shut. Downstairs he poured himself a whisky; I didn't want one or need one. I suppose it would be a bit of a shock before you got used to Violet. He sat across from me at the oak table, glancing out of the window towards the power station every now and then. It glowed in the cloudy night. And I told him everything, from the beginning. He nodded sometimes, refilled his whisky, sometimes squeezed my fingertips where my hand rested on the tabletop.

"So, you found the driftwood last October gone, the night of the storm?"

"That's right – well the morning after."

He looked hard at me and said, "I think Seb and I saw it too, earlier that morning, or late in the night, glowing like you said. I hadn't realised it was the same driftwood you brought in…I hadn't thought. It was so mad that night. Then Granny Irene…"

"The thing is, I need your help, Solomon. I think she wants to get home, that's what she's trying to tell me. She's already helped the Headland; we must help her."

I tried to explain about the images. "Will you come back in a few days, come back and take her out with me, and we can figure out how to get her home?"

He took one more swig and put the cap back on the whisky, placed both his big hands over mine and leant closer over the table. "I will help you, Dolly. You know I will."

I sighed. "I know you won't let me down, Solomon. You never have. Let's not tell anyone else – I don't think she would be safe. You know how people around here can be. And Seb, I know he's your brother but not Seb because of what's been happening."

"You can trust me, Dolores."

He said very little after that. He needed to go. He told me to be careful, that perhaps I should sleep downstairs tonight. I told him I was perfectly safe. Violet would never hurt me. He looked briefly towards the staircase before he headed for the door, as if he might go back up there for another look at my beautiful Violet, spinning the universe through her heart.

At the door, I said, "Sol, about you leaving with Seb: I understand, but I want you to know I feel the same. I want you to come back to me…I'll see you in a few days then, anyway?"

He simply nodded and was gone again, the late blooms in Watchbell's nighttime garden bowing solemnly in his wake.

There are only a few pages left of the diary. Morgan does not skip to the end, though. He is getting ready to leave Watchbell House and breaks off from his reading to throw away the old bottles and tins, wrap the canvases and load his car. He decides to leave the painting of the mermaid's purse above the fireplace. He stands in front of it for a long while, trying to see beneath the layers of dark, velvety oil paint. Then he mops the floorboards and cleans the sink, washes the bedding and hangs it in the tidied garden where it flaps whitely in the breeze. He stands for a while in the porch gazing out at the calm, green sea. People wander the beach with their dogs and children, heading for the pub, or the ice cream van, or a trip on the narrow-gauge train that chugs along every hour. He turns to look at the power station, squat and blank in the distance, to be closed down next year, unless the campaigners have their way. Odd to think of it staying there, not making energy, the birds roosting on its false cliff face. It is time to say goodbye, so he locks the yellow door and heads towards the Squid Studio and Gallery.

As he nears it, he sees in dripping black spray paint, scrawled across its whitewashed boards, the words: *KEEP INVADERS OFF OUR COAST. DON'T HARBOUR ILLEGAL IMMIGRANTS.* The right-wing group are gathered around the sea mine at the shore, this time all dressed in heavy black, their faces red and beaded with sweat. The door to the gallery is not open, but Claire is at the top of the dunes, the breeze lifting the curls away from her face, coming down from Café Ferdinand, her keys dangling in her hand. She sees the writing before he can warn her, and her pace quickens. She slips down the sandy path as it turns to shingle, and comes raging towards him, face twisted.

"You bastards!" she shouts over his head. "This was my father's house. He would never stop helping people, and neither will I."

Morgan grabs her arm as she runs past him, stops her, almost lifts her off the ground. "They aren't worth it, Claire," he says close and softly into her ear. She crumples, as though the run down the dunes used up the only energy she had left. The men are laughing at them, grinning and muttering to one another. Morgan holds Claire into his torso and turns her away from the shore so she can't see them. He faces them. Suddenly they scatter away from the sea mine. Half go west, the others east, dashing along the shingle.

"We warned you," one calls over his shoulder.

Morgan frowns, holding Claire close, and looks at the sea mine. It is glowing underneath as if fringed with candles. It is defunct as the skull of a beached whale, green, rusted and decorated with barnacles. It doesn't have any fuses and has been checked and double-checked for safety over the years. But, Morgan realises, there are new bombs beneath it.

"What the –?" he mutters as it explodes, shattering into a thousand salty pieces. The sky shifts and the sea spins upwards. The white boards of the studio split apart and fly towards Morgan and Claire, slicing through their bodies where they stand holding one another. Morgan feels it, not as pain, but as a dissolving of his atoms; they drift away from him as his mother's ashes did on the wind. The blue horizon darkens to indigo and the spinning water forms a tunnel, a weird umbilical through which he can see another Headland, another shore. But it is night there, stars puncturing the black sky. At the other end he glimpses figures standing on the dark beach, and one looks like his mother in the photographs, her brown hair tumbling down her back, her almond eyes searching his own across an impossible distance. Claire's warm blood is spattered all over him. The beach is strewn with the bodies of holidaymakers, and men in black clothes who did not realise how powerful their bombs were, how they would activate the old explosives in the sea mine and make shrapnel of it. The old lighthouse is shattered, glass from its top raining brightly onto the viper's bugloss. The seakale smells of burnt sugar.

A blast echoes around the beach. As his body dissipates, huge wings fold down to envelop what is left of his consciousness. He is in a cave of plush darkness. He breathes in the scent of smoking lemons. This is a new experience, and yet he feels at home…As if he is returning to a place long forgotten.

Then, in a split second, with a rush of air on his face and a pain in his chest, everything is sucked back into the sea mine: the blood; the fragmented wooden boards; the glass; Morgan himself.

There is a great pressure, and he is released. Breathless, he looks towards the sea mine. It is covered by a winged shape that pulses with phosphorescence. The shape unfurls: a huge organic contraption fletched with velvet, wearing a face like every face and no face he has ever seen. The face is suddenly his mother's, before she was ever ill. Then the creature wears Morgan's face. Then Solomon's death mask. Then a terrified boy, soaked by the sea. Then Claire's face. Then Maggie's.

The wings open and unfold until the summer sky is in shadow, and then they beat and their beat sounds around the shore and the force of their beating blows the hair back from Morgan's brow. With that breeze against his skin, he realises he has skin, he has a body, he is intact. Unexploded. The creature rises, huge, over the sea, until it is far away, a form on the horizon that could be an albatross, or a bat, or an errant storm.

Nothing has changed.

Everything has.

His mother is dead. Her ashes floated out onto the sea. He closed the door on her body as it lay like a wax copy in the hospital bed. And yet she still lives, she is warm and breathing, somewhere in some loop of time, at the end of this impossible tunnel, this hole exploded in the universe.

There is a place where Solomon stands on his boat, hauling in turquoise nets that jostle with crabs.

There is a place where Morgan is yet to be. A place where he unspools in the darkness as his own child is now unspooling in the darkness.

There is a place where Morgan is already a father with a creamy, slippery child in his arms, her face a reflection of all the faces that have existed before her. He is cutting the tough gristle of her umbilical cord, meeting her slate-blue eyes as they roll towards him in recognition.

There is also a place where Morgan is gone and not returning, where his blood seeps like oil into the shingle, where he is not saved.

All of this is happening right now.

Nothing has changed. Everything has.

With a jolt, he crashes onto the beach backwards and finds he is sitting on the shingle, stunned, looking up at a lone white cloud drifting in the blue sky.

"Morgan? Are you alright?" says Claire, who stands above him, shielding her eyes with her hand. "You just…fell down. Did you faint?"

Sharp stones cut into his legs and palms. He frowns up at Claire, older than him, kinder and wiser. Alive. This time, it was more than just an episode. The fabric of his life seems to have been ripped open, and then just as suddenly restitched.

He doesn't know what to say and stammers out: "I think I just…slipped…I'm sorry."

"Don't be sorry," she says, taking his arm and hauling him onto his feet. "Where did those guys go?"

Morgan looks up and down the beach but can see no sign of them in their black clothes.

"I'm not sure. But good riddance."

After what has just happened, he wants to pretend to be normal. He says, "Listen, I'll help you clean the writing off the studio. We can sort it out."

"Thanks, Morgan. I think I overreacted. Shall we get a drink? I feel a bit…weird."

Morgan dusts himself down. His head feels wobbly, as if it's not quite connected to his body.

"Yes. Good idea. And no, I don't think you overreacted," he says softly.

Friday 16th September 1988. Noon.

Things didn't happen as I had thought. Solomon came back the next evening just as I was about to take Violet on a walk to the sea mine. She was hovering about my head, her great creaking wings outstretched and almost covering the entire ceiling, when Sol opened the door without knocking. I smiled to see him; Sol was as good as his word, believing me and coming to help Violet. It was already dark outside, some frayed clouds illuminated to grey by the moon, shortly after a rain shower, the garden lavender scented. But Solomon had two men with him; they emerged like his own shadow dividing itself behind him. One was the man from the plant, Clement, whom I had met about the confiscated driftwood, in his morbid dark suit; the other was my doctor, squat with a smug yet impassive face, whom I had not seen for almost two years. The last time I saw him, he said, "You can always try again…" and I hated him for it and vowed never to lay eyes on him in the future. I couldn't breathe for a moment. I didn't recognise the expression on Sol's face.

"Dolores," he said softly, raising his palms in front of him, "let us come in."

"Right then," said the doctor briskly, "we need to sit you on the sofa."

And Clement looked up at Violet floating like a canopy above my head and reached for her. "I don't see," he muttered to Solomon over his angular shoulder, "quite what you're getting at."

As they moved into Watchbell House – my house – I looked beyond them out of the open door and saw a silhouette just before the boundary of my garden: Seb, out there on the shingle, waiting. At the moment the doctor reached for my arm, Violet folded her great, black wings down to envelop me. I couldn't see anything and smelt the sugary underside of her furred wings. I was lifted slightly from the ground and knew from the cool night air that she had taken me from the house.

The men ran, calling, after us. Her wings opened, brushing my skin as she released me onto the beach, and she soared away from me. As she did, the doctor and Clement made a grab for her, the doctor for a moment hanging from the delicate membrane of one of her wings and tearing a hole in it. He fell on the shingle and she flew away from him with an awkward beat, listing at an angle in the sky.

"Don't hurt her, for God's sake!" screamed out Solomon.

The scraps of cloud were clearing, and stars smattered the blackness. The men could run, but they would never catch her. She made her way to the shore, moonlight shining in her feathery fur, her body still flashing with those repeated images: Watchbell House, sea mine, snail shell, fishing boat. Seb was closest to her, but she reached the sea mine before he could get near. She landed on its barnacled, old metal surface and wrapped herself over it, remnant of the war, reminder of what we do to each other in hatred and fear. She began to pulse with light, her darkness transforming into brightness and a keening cry from deep inside her went out across the sea. The earth rumbled, the sea mine shrieked like a living thing, and then it exploded.

I had time to think, *But the fuses?*, and to realise that somehow Violet had detonated the bomb. It was so bright, but as I looked beyond it, looked *through* it (as I had learnt to do when I first encountered Violet), I saw the sea had risen into a twister, a vortex of water that spiralled like a shell, tunnelling away from us. Down that tunnel of water, at the other side, I saw the Headland, but in daylight, a mirror of our own shoreline, and a distant figure standing there that I recognised but could not place. I looked behind me: Watchbell House was in the process of shattering into a thousand splinters of tarred timber, the garden decimated and the power station in the distance behind just one impossible ball of light.

Then the explosion retracted for a moment, as if caught in a tide, and none of these things happened at all; it receded into Violet's heart and was gone.

Then it burst away from her again, violent and deafening, shards of bomb and fishing boats, tiny stones and the remnants of crabs, Seb's limbs and flesh spattering over the shingle, the other men vanishing in the flames, the tunnel of water spiralling over the sea with the weird double of the Headland visible at the end of it. And me, I shattered too, dissipated into a billion pieces, turning to ash on the wind, and with me all sense of time, all sense of feeling. There was no pain, I only felt calm, I only thought, *here we go...*

Then the explosion sucked back in again and I felt a sharp, unbearable pain in my centre which lasted only a second, then it all rewound into Violet, and she shrank and disappeared into the night in a pinpoint of darkness. The beach was still; the sea mine was inert and intact. I was sitting on the stones. Violet was gone.

My shoulder hurt, as if it had been jerked out of its socket. Solomon came to sit beside me, rubbing his jaw, his eyebrows knotted together. The doctor was shaking his head. "Let's get you inside, Mrs Poole," he said as Sol helped me up. His voice sounded as though it was coming to me from underwater. Clement stood with his thin suit flapping in the sea breeze, looking at me, then Seb. "I don't think I'm needed here, Mr Marston, why don't you see me back to my car?" They both took a glance at the horizon, the drift of the Milky Way intermittently concealed by cloud. I stumbled back into Watchbell House, shrugging Solomon off me, telling the doctor I had not called for him and he need not stay.

"But Mrs Poole, your arm..." It throbbed, and I noticed the jumper my mother had knitted for me was torn at the shoulder with a thin scrape of blood as from someone's nail on the exposed skin.

"It's fine," I replied, shocked tears rising in my throat. "I don't want you to touch it." My hearing was humming from the explosion that both did and did not happen, was always happening and, thanks to Violet, never would. I hoped they understood she'd saved them from being obliterated and I glimpsed from their expressions that in some way, they did.

Morgan reads the entry over and over, trying to understand how his mother had experienced an explosion too. He thinks of asking Maggie about it – perhaps there is some plausible physical explanation. But his head hurts at the idea, and he wonders if instead he has already read this entry, forgotten as he fell asleep. It has been stressful and sad; he had not expected another death, just the tying up of his mother's life, a goodbye to the Headland forever. He has drunk too much from the old bottle of whisky. Now, he is not so sure about anything. Not the creature, Violet, and her second, dark incarnation.

And least of all his mother's journal, itself a twisting tunnel of water and stars and darkness – a tunnel leading from her to him and back again.

Sunday 2nd October 1988, 7.07 p.m.

The days spin by without Violet. I'm back at school, teaching again. Claire looks so grown up after this summer, her long curls cut short. I watch the curve of her jaw clenching as she concentrates on her ink drawings. This is her final year of sixth form; I'm helping her with her application to art school. I can still paint; I have not had a block since I first met Violet. My oil piece of the mermaid's purse now hangs above the hearth, one corner slightly crushed where it twice fell to the ground. Though I didn't try to paint the moving shapes beneath its skin, in a certain light it shines as if to suggest there is something inside it. I've almost finished the triptych too, adding an obscure, explosive light to the edge of the power station. The garden begins to fade, only the Michaelmas daisies and a few anemones blooming, delicate purple amongst the flame red of the fruitless blueberry bushes.

It's Sunday, so I went to see my mother. The lilac trees lining the path to the home are losing their leaves. I approached Mum from behind where she sat in the conservatory, blanket over her knees, wisps of grey hair curled at her neck, her neck a delicate stem. Windfall apples poked their bare heads from the lawn. I walked around and took my mother's hand, feeling the bones under the loose skin.

"Mum."

"Dolores. Dolly-mixture mine; look at you." Her voice sounded mucousy in her throat, but the nurse said she was doing well; the chest infection was responding to treatment. She had something folded in her lap.

"I've brought some ginger cake today," I told her. The butter was soaking through the brown paper bag. "They're making us some tea to go with it."

"Lovely." She gazed beyond me, out of the window where a dry breeze knocked a few more leaves off the trees. They twisted onto the lawn like flames going out.

"You know, I like autumn," she said, "the way it reminds you nothing stays the same, there is always a shift. Things go and then come back."

"I suppose so," I said, pulling a chair up beside her. I didn't let go of her hand.

"I've made something for you." She passed me the clothes she'd knitted which were there on her lap. A green hat, tiny and soft. A cardigan in green and yellow, the stitching in intricate, careful stripes. Little boots that tie with a woollen bow. They must have taken weeks, or even months. Not a single mistake. Not a single dropped stitch or loose thread.

"But, Mum, you do remember what happened?"

She looked hard at me, her dark eyes fading to pale olive and rheumy, her cheeks pink and papery, her mouth set.

"I do remember, Dolores. But this gift is for you now. Things have changed."

My face was hot – I didn't know where Mum was in time. I took a deep breath and sliced into the cake.

Saturday 15th October 1988. Afternoon.

Almost a year, I realise, since this journal began. A year since the storm.

The sea froths grey and silver out on the horizon and the wind gets colder. I walk the beach slowly now, looking for driftwood and shells. I found a shell today, grubby and crusted on the outside but a corridor of mother-of-pearl when I held it up to my eye. I lit the fire last night, the first time since summer faded. I was out in the garden this morning dead-heading the roses and turning the soil over in the bare beds, cutting the gorse back from the window. My fingernails are filled with earth and I smell of iron and salt. This time of year is hard, and takes me back to thoughts of you. Tomorrow it will be two years since I saw your lovely face.

I saw Solomon from a distance, knew him by his loping stride up the beach. There was something cradled in his arms, a fish I thought at first. I kept on pruning and weeding, the wind carrying my hair over my eyes. When he reached the garden, I saw he was holding a bouquet of white irises, their yellow eyes like yolks amongst the ghostly petals. He held them towards me.

"Where did you get these?" I said, wrapping my hand around their damp stems. "Quite a find at this time of year."

"I know someone, cultivates them." His voice was gruff. His eyes turned to the lighthouse. "Fog might come in. Bloody foghorn'll be on later I reckon. Shouldn't complain I suppose."

I smiled and nestled the irises into my chest. He squared his feet to mine.

"I came because tomorrow is an important anniversary. I wanted you to know I'll be thinking of you," he said.

"Thank you," I replied, though I don't know if he heard me as the words clogged in my throat; I didn't know he had remembered the date.

"Can you forgive me, Dolly, for what happened on the beach?"

I thought of Violet, the tear in her wing as she swooped away down to the shore.

"You promised me you'd help me, that you wouldn't tell anyone. I trusted you, Solomon."

He looked down at his feet, clad in their rubber boots, then back up to my face.

"I was so worried about you, Dolores. I was trying to help you."

"Well, she's gone now, so I suppose it doesn't matter anymore."

"She?"

"The creature, whoever she was and wherever she was from. You saw her – she was beautiful."

He frowned, those black, bushy brows shading his eyes.

He paused, then put his hand on my arm for a moment. "Listen, I also came to tell you something: I'm going with Seb to the city, just until he gets on his feet. But…do you want me to be back here, as soon as I can get back?" He glanced down at my body and back to my face.

I saw in his eyes that he did not believe he had ever seen Violet. Perhaps this was because of the men he brought with him that night, because they explained her away as some wild animal or mutant affected by the power station. In that moment, I couldn't forgive him. Solomon who'd loved me, who'd tamed the wild sea and brought me shimmering fish and held me in the dark – that Solomon had been mine. But this one had broken his promise.

"I will be alright on my own, Sol. Look after your brother, he needs you."

I shifted the irises to the crook of my arm, reached up and kissed him goodbye.

Sunday 16th October 1988. Morning.

It was October 16th, 1986. Two years ago. A Thursday. One year exactly before the storm. The storm became a dark anniversary. But I won't forget the date. I never will.

You weren't due to be born for three weeks, but I felt this unloosening in my back, and by mid-morning my waters had broken. Adrian and I had decided to spend the weekend at Watchbell House and I was looking at the garden at the time: purple Michaelmas daisies, ragwort, driftwood, unruly, honey-scented seakale. I wondered at first where the liquid had come from. It shimmered on the stones, slightly iridescent like the skin of a soap bubble, and kept trickling out of me. I called the midwife, who didn't seem worried; you were a bit early but full-term.

I kept pacing back and forth to the garden, like a wild animal that wanted to be outside, but felt safer inside. The pains in my back became more intense, crushing, making me stand still and just stare at the sea, which was tipped with white, wobbling.

I went inside and sat on the floor in the front room, trying to steady my breath. I kept thinking of you and how I would meet you soon. Adrian came back from town where he'd been getting supplies for the weekend. I saw chocolate, matches, lemons, poking from the shopping bag.

The clouds darkened, grew heavy and began to spit with rain. At some point the rain became torrential. I lost all sense of time, sometimes I was gone for hours, phasing away and only coming back when someone spoke to me.

Adrian was smiling, his lips moving. I batted him away when he touched me. I felt too quivering and delicate to be touched, as though the boundary of my skin was gone. I couldn't hear what he said, but I saw he was excited about becoming a father, trembling with anticipation. The midwife was there, her face fading in and out of focus.

At times the small front room of the house seemed miles long, and she far away in the corner of it. And for some reason, Solomon was there, in the doorway like a shadow. I discovered later that the midwife had called out for directions, just as he was hauling his catch across the shingle. He had stayed in case he was needed. Smelling of brine and the metallic air.

I saw my bare knees, then I heard the directive to push. I had things I wanted to say, but they just blew around my head and wouldn't come out.

Far away, a woman screamed.

There was a breaking inside my body, as of a huge door being opened, or bone moving aside for the first time, a hot pressure that I needed to bear against, and then you slithered free and were lifted up. I glimpsed your skin, slick with chalky vernix, a whorl of pale hair at your crown. I waited for your cry, your first breath...

I feel as though I have been waiting for that breath my entire life.

The midwife was blue-white, her smile erased. She rubbed you with a towel. She asked in a strangled voice for someone to call an ambulance. Adrian didn't move. His hands were up at either side of his head, as if he were holding it on. He stepped backwards. He looked through the rain-blurred window to the horizon. But there was no escape. Solomon strode through the doorway and grabbed the phone. He looked enormous. Everyone did somehow. Your own tiny limbs red-grey. Your fingernails like petals. I reached up to you, connected to me still by your twisting umbilical. My breasts felt hot with milk. The midwife put you on my chest, then looked away, biting her lip. Your umbilical, thick and silky, brushing against my fingers. The line that joined us, like fisherman to catch.

As I held you, all of your heat seeped into me. I think now how we are our own heat, leaving its trace as we pass though time. I wanted to send it back to you. I wanted to turn cold as stone so that you might suddenly gasp into life. But heat only moves one way. Your mouth was puckered in a silent kiss. You were soft and damp. You were mine. I had never really thought about the idea of a heart breaking, that cliché phrase, but I felt it then, a great cracking in my chest, a heavy pain like I had been cut open and a rock put inside me. Adrian was speaking, every phrase a question. There were blue lights outside the doorway. I tried to ignore it all and listen to the sea raking at the stones, the gulls crying. I held you tight, your face, squashed in your passage through my body, settling now into peace. The trace of your eyebrows. Your look of unconcern. You'd squirmed and kicked in my stretched body all those months, but you were silent now. I would never watch you becoming.

They let me hold you for a long time, until your head felt like a little ball of stone. Until the sky darkened to indigo in the square of the window and the Milky Way appeared. I wondered if you experienced me at all. If you had time to catch my scent, or the feel of my skin against you, to hear my heartbeat from the outside as you had for so long safe on the inside. I still wonder what your brief seconds on earth felt like. I hope you felt loved and were not afraid.

There wasn't a reason, or none they could discover. These things happen, they said. These things happen. I could try again, in time. But I kept seeing only you. Adrian looked for answers, trying to blame: the midwife, the doctors, even me. And then he wanted another baby, with an obsessive desire as if that could solve everything. When it didn't happen, when month after month I bled, I felt strangely relieved. Eventually he wanted to be anywhere but near me. I wanted to be here, at Watchbell House. My blood stains still on the floorboards. They comfort me but are too much for him.

We scattered your ashes at sea. Solomon took us on his boat so we could be sure you'd go right out, on the wind. And in a way, that's the last time your father and I were really together. Who can blame him? Grief takes us in different ways. It's the same as grief for an older person, but more: it's also grief for the life you thought you were going to have, undefined as it might have been. You, my love, should have been part of it. We kept hearing the fuzzy sound of the name we had chosen for you. Adrian daren't speak it. But I whispered it from time to time into the wind on the beach: *Iris. Iris.* My mother's middle name. Flower of the damp earth. Goddess of the rainbow. *Iris.*

For a while after, my breasts leaked milk and, whenever I was in town, I saw new babies and pregnant women everywhere, as if they had multiplied overnight just to torment me. I felt a raging jealousy, a hatred that turned itself back on me. Sometimes I'd drop my shopping and leave wherever I was with it still at the till, half rung up, bemused cashiers calling after me. I understood that life is fragile and that everyone dies, but I didn't know how to grieve for you. You had died before you lived, died on the day you were born. Life and death should not coexist in that way. It was as if time itself had collapsed, the future crashing into the present so that nothing could run its course. I couldn't work out how to mourn the future.

I lay in bed at night, staring at the rafters, bargaining with a god I don't believe in. I would have set fire to the world to have you live an hour more.

I found I couldn't trust my senses. I looked around at the Headland and saw the fraying clouds; the egg-shaped pebbles on the beach; the grey-blue sea; the wrecked and the still-working fishing boats; people walking their dogs. But it felt unreal, it didn't exist. The pylons threaded away from the power station and into the distance, the black lighthouse looked like a rocket about to take off, the narrow-gauge train clattered past. A child in a striped coat waved at me from one of the carriages, and I raised my hand but could not smile. I lost faith in what I saw. The breeze ran over my skin and I couldn't feel it anymore.

Solomon spoke to me now and again. He could look me in the eye and ask how I was; he had been there. He had seen you. I longed to ask him about you, to see if he remembered your sweet face. But I felt I couldn't, that he would want to forget.

One afternoon, Randy came over. I was lying on the sofa, half-asleep but not able to drop off. She knocked gently then pushed open the unlocked door.

"I need your help," she said as I lifted myself up. In her jacket was a furry bundle, mewling, trembling and digging its claws into her chest. "Last of the litter. No-one wants him because he's bigger than the others. Uglier I guess. Never heard of such a thing: I always thought the runt was the outcast. But look at me, I suppose…What do I know anyway? So, he's going to stay here and keep you company.

Where's the coffee? We both need some. Not the cat – me and you."

The kitten was in my arms with his big, unruly bat ears, and Randy was in the kitchen. My only thought was: *Oh no, now I can't be left alone to die. Now I have to stay alive.* I tried many times to give Wotsit back, taking him to the café and begging. Randy ignored me each time and poured me a tea and gave me a sandwich I could not eat. One day, when Wotsit was sitting on my lap and I was kneading his fur, I forgot to think of it, forgot to go and take him back, just kept stroking him.

I returned to work, smiling at the students and showing them how to approach the lines of a still life or landscape, wash their brushes and mix their paints. I avoided the staffroom. Often if I met a colleague, they did not know what to say and I felt responsible for their embarrassment. At home I sobbed and slept, dreaming about you, hearing your name in my ears, though you were often in the guise of a mammal, an amphibian, a bee, a flower – any living thing I had failed to look after. I couldn't paint at all because all I saw was your delicate body, the wrinkles on your new, slippery skin, your tiny eyelashes. I knew exactly how to paint them, but to do so seemed a kind of sacrilege.

I've written to you, Iris, as if you might know my words, but I realise you are only a memory, an idea. I didn't know how to mourn someone, the most important someone in the world, who died before they could live. But after what has happened in the two years that have followed your birth, I think I understand. After what happened to Violet, I have glimpsed that time might not be what we imagine. That we just can't really see how it works. That we are all always already dying and already being born; somehow everything is happening all the time. But we can only land on a little bit of time, like a butterfly on a leaf. I have let your death live in me. Death is another transformation. I have let mourning into me so that you will always be there, but I can carry on living. Grief is a dark gift. I can let you go, and at the same time love you always.

And now another baby is coming. I am heavy with it. Planetary. It won't be long. The sea air tastes metallic. I can smell the burnt sugar scent of the seakale turning. My hips click as I walk. I lie awake at night holding my breath for kicks and pushes against the inside of my skin. Who knows what he or she will be like? Are any of us fully human anyway? I am afraid, but I will always be afraid because I want breath, I want life in those tiny limbs. You will never be forgotten or replaced, but I feel life coming to me out of nowhere, out of the universe. The heart beating, the skin thickening, the little brain firing. Maybe I will recognise their face as if I had always known them, as I recognised you. Or maybe they will be a stranger. Not of this world.

Morgan's birthday is the 20th of October 1988, just a few days later. There are no more diary entries, just blank pages. He realises now that the diary was addressed to the baby lost a year before his mother began writing. His elder sister. The diary is a love letter. He is none the wiser about the truth of Violet, and at the same time understands that she is real. Real as a force, like the energy of a storm. She saved his mother, and he thinks she may have saved him in some way too. He isn't sure how. Not yet. But time will tell.

Claire is at the top of the loft ladder, shining a torch into the dark.

"I don't see any bats in here…" Her feet disappear into the hatch and Morgan follows her up. The loft is almost empty. He expected to discover more secrets, but there are only thick cobwebs and a couple of empty boxes. He stoops down near the hatch. Claire sits on the boards and shines the torch into the eaves. There are some old bat droppings, virtually fossilised, and a small, white skull. Morgan collects this and puts it onto his palm.

"Alas, poor Yorick…"

"Yorick's a good name for a deceased bat; he'll look nice in the garden," laughs Claire. She shines the torch under her chin. "Do you remember the time Dad had a massive beehive in his roof? I'm sure you were there."

Morgan thinks back to when Squid Studio was Solomon's fishing cottage. In summers they'd go to collect nets and bait for the boat, life jackets for him and Claire.

"You must have been about five or six, because I was back from uni. Dad knew there was a hive up in the roof, and he was live-and-let-live about it. But he had no idea how huge it was. One day, the honeycomb collapsed the roof, and bees and honey came pouring out."

Now, Morgan remembers. It is the smell that comes back: musky, too sweet, like hot human skin. And the vibration of thousands of bees, their fuzzy universe erupting into his own, all of them swirling around him. Honey and rooftiles everywhere.

"We were all flapping about, covered in bees, terrified," says Claire. "But not you. You stood there cool as a cucumber, with a cloud of them around your head. We all got stung a few times, but they didn't touch you. Even though you broke off a bit of honeycomb before your mum could stop you."

Morgan can see the beautiful architecture of those tiny chambers, each with subtly different colours inside them.

"Yes," he says, "I do remember that."

She says, "I guess we should close this hatch now."

Downstairs, leaning against the kitchen worktop, he says to Claire, "There's something I want to ask you."

"Oh yes?"

"Will you look after Watchbell House for me?" He pushes the keys across the empty counter.

"I thought you wanted to sell it."

"I've changed my mind. I want to visit in the summers. With my family."

"Your family? I didn't know…" smiles Claire, surprised and delighted. Morgan flushes, as if he's trying on an outfit that's too big for him.

"My girlfriend is about to have our baby. I think she'd like it here, and the little one would too. I know I did. I know that, now I've been back…"

Claire squeezes his arm. "That's brilliant, Morgan, congratulations. I'll look after the house for you, I promise. I might have to find a gardener though."

They both laugh.

Morgan says, "I'm going to leave most of the paintings. You can keep them."

Claire raises her eyebrows. "You sure, Morgan?"

"I'm sure."

"I'd love to put on an exhibition."

"I'd love that too."

They fall silent for a while, and both glance towards the painting of the mermaid's purse hanging darkly above the fireplace. Morgan turns to Claire, his breath suddenly shallow.

"Claire, can I ask you, do you remember my mother before I was born? Do you think she was ever…was there anything about her that struck you as…?" He flounders.

"Morgan." She looks him hard in the eye. "I was a teenager, so everything was weird to me. But what I can tell you about your mother is this: she loved deeply, she felt deeply. She wasn't like everyone else; she saw different kinds of truths and shapes in the world. That's what made her a good artist. She was the way we should all be."

Morgan smiles. This doesn't answer his question, but he's satisfied nonetheless.

"So, you off today then?" asks Claire.

"I thought I would stay for Solomon's funeral."

"That's not for two weeks, Morgan; you know how these things go. Besides, you have a baby on the way; you need to get back to your girlfriend."

"Are you sure, Claire?"

She puts her arm around his shoulder, and he leans down to make it easier. Her muscles are delicate but deceptively strong. "You've been to enough funerals for one summer," she whispers.

"One last bacon butty for you, Morgan Poole," says Randy as he walks into Café Ferdinand. "I saw you parking your car. Egg on the side. Sweet black coffee."

"Thanks, Randy."

She sits opposite him in the booth, looking brighter than a few days ago.

"Funny thing," she says. "These right-wing characters – I haven't seen them in a few days. Height of summer, they're always here. Don't like me, call me all the names under the sun when they think I can't hear them, but sure like my fry-ups. But the last few days, I haven't seen hide nor hair…"

"Funny," says Morgan, through a mouthful of bacon.

Randy holds his forearm, lightly, from across the table.

"Will I see you again soon here? You know how decrepit I'm getting…"

Morgan smiles. "You are not. And you will see me. I'll come back and stay in Watchbell House soon. I won't be away so long this time."

"Good lad."

Randy never charges him for food, but on the way out, Morgan reaches into his pocket and leaves a bright spill of change.

He leans on the car bonnet and looks to the horizon. Calm, grey-edged waves; two lighthouses, one working, one not, and the hulk of the power station. Cottages and studios, every one of them different to the next, lining the beach. Wrecked boats and working machinery. The old sea mine, like a washed-up memory. The enormous sky, which in a few hours will turn dark blue and show the dusting of the Milky Way, its lights the elegies of stars.

His phone rings. It is Maggie, breathless, calling from the city:

"M…Morgan," she says.

"Maggie?"

"You…" She breathes heavily between words, as if they are being dragged back into her throat. "You know I said… first…babies…are always…late?" For a moment, the contraction passes and her voice steadies. "Well, this one seems to be on its way."

Maggie, clever Maggie studying time and heat and physics, is going to have their baby soon. Morgan drops his phone, then catches it with his other hand before it hits the ground.

"Don't…panic…" She blows her breath out, as though trying to control a storm that is passing through her. "I think…you have…a couple of…hours…"

A smile breaks across Morgan's face. Clouds gather in the summer sky, banking up in deep greys and honey-yellows.

He takes one last look at the Headland's stark horizon. For a moment, his dark eyes catch the light and flash violet.

"I'm coming, Maggie," he says. "I'm going to be there."

Acknowledgements

I would like to thank the following people for supporting me whilst I wrote this book: my husband, Miles (also a brilliant editor); my agent, Donald Winchester, for belief in my work; my creative and beautiful friends and colleagues with whom I have had conversations about this book: Naomi Booth, Kimberly Campanello, Anne-Marie Evans, Liesl King, Kaley Kramer, Rob Edgar, Sam Reese, Nicholas Royle and Rob O'Connor. I am forever grateful to my family for encouraging my wild imagination and to my brother Simon for a shared love of science fiction.

I also want to say thank you to the brilliant editorial team at Gold SF, Una McCormack, Paul March-Russell and Aliya Whiteley in particular.

Watchbell House is based loosely on Derek Jarman's Prospect Cottage. I was greatly inspired by his descriptions of the changing landscape of Dungeness in his journal *Modern Nature*. A number of other texts were inspirations for *The Headland*, including William Shakespeare's *The Tempest*, the writings of physicist Carlo Rovelli, the *Refugee Tales* anthologies edited by David Herd, fiction by Ted Chiang and Jeff VanderMeer, L. Frank Baum's *The Wizard of Oz*, the films of John Carpenter, Nicolas Roeg and Denis Villeneuve, and the flower poems of Alice Oswald.

COPYRIGHT ACKNOWLEDGEMENTS

The Michael Fish 1987 BBC Weather quotation is reproduced with permission of the BBC.